HEART OF FIRE

Louise Cooper was born in Hertfordshire in 1952. She hated school so much — spending most lessons clandestinely writing stories — that she persuaded her parents to let her abandon her education at the age of fifteen and has never regretted it. Her first novel was published when she was twenty. She moved to London in 1975 and worked in publishing before becoming a full-time writer in 1977. Since then she has published more than twenty fantasy novels, for both adults and children, and has ideas for many more to come. She also writes occasional short stories, and poetry for her own pleasure.

Louise Cooper lives in an area sandwiched between the Cotswolds and the Malverns and gains a great deal of inspiration from the scenery. She is also potty about cats and steam trains!

Heart of Fire was previously published as *Firespell* in the Dark Enchantment series.

Heart of Fire

Louise Cooper

PUFFIN BOOKS

PUFFIN BOOKS

Published by the Penguin Group
Penguin Books Ltd, 27 Wrights Lane, London W8 5TZ, England
Penguin Putnam Inc., 375 Hudson Street, New York, New York 10014, USA
Penguin Books Australia Ltd, Ringwood, Victoria, Australia
Penguin Books Canada Ltd, 10 Alcorn Avenue, Toronto, Ontario, Canada M4V 3B2
Penguin Books (NZ) Ltd, 182–190 Wairau Road, Auckland 10, New Zealand

Penguin Books Ltd, Registered Offices: Harmondsworth, Middlesex, England

First published in Puffin Books 1996
Reissued in this edition 1998
1 3 5 7 9 10 8 6 4 2

Copyright © Louise Cooper, 1996

All rights reserved

The moral right of the author has been asserted

Typeset in 12/15 Plantin

Made and printed in England by Clays Ltd, St Ives plc

British Library Cataloguing in Publication Data
A CIP catalogue record for this book is available from the British Library

ISBN 0-140-38771-4

Chapter One

PRIDDY CAME INTO the turret room that Lianne shared with her sister, Gretala, and her voice was very quiet as she said, 'Your grandmother wants to see you.'

Lianne and Gretala exchanged an uneasy look. Grandmother had been ill for some time, and lately the servants had begun to whisper that her sickness was growing worse. The apothecary called every day, and there was a sinister hush in the west wing where Grandmother's room was. Now, seeing their old nurse's serious face, the girls knew the truth.

'Yes,' Priddy nodded sombrely. 'Your grandmother is dying. The apothecary says she will make the great journey before nightfall, so you must go to her and say your goodbyes.' She beckoned them towards the door. 'Come along, now.'

Lianne's face grew stricken. 'To the west wing . . .?' she whispered.

'Yes.' Then Priddy's expression softened. 'There's nothing to fear there. Only shadows, and they can't hurt anyone. Come, now. No dawdling.'

Lianne tried very hard not to think about shadows as she and Gretala followed Priddy's bobbing candle to the west wing. The corridors were chill and gloomy, and outside the wind was rising. It moaned eerily, and all the windows had started to rattle, as if a hundred ghouls were trying to prise them open and get into the house. On the walls, portraits of the Cerne family ancestors watched the girls hurry by. Lianne didn't dare look at the faces in the pictures. They were all grim in the brightest daylight; on this hideous autumn evening they would be nightmarish.

Lord and Lady Cerne were waiting outside Grandmother's door. Lady Cerne looked as if she had been crying, and Lord Cerne didn't greet his daughters but only said, 'Your grandmother is waiting for you. She wants to see you one at a time. Lianne, you are to go first.'

Lianne's heart missed a beat. She didn't want to be first, and she looked at Gretala in appeal. But Lord Cerne frowned and said sternly, 'Lianne, did you hear me?'

She swallowed and dropped an obedient curtsy. 'Yes, Father.' And, taking a deep breath, she reached out for the door handle.

'*Lianne . . . is that Lianne?*'

The voice sounded like the rustling of dead leaves, so feeble and thin that Lianne could barely hear it. 'Yes, Grandmother,' she whispered back.

'Ah, I can see your hair now. Your handsome auburn hair . . . Come closer, child. Stand in the light, where I can also see your face.'

Lianne tiptoed towards the huge, curtained bed. Six candles burned in a branched sconce on a table, but the light they gave was weak and pale. An elderly maid sat in a chair by the empty fireplace, apparently asleep. The room was very cold. And the wind outside was howling now, like a damned soul.

Grandmother lay propped up by pillows, looking tiny and lost among all the whiteness. Lianne dropped a deeper curtsy. She felt she should say something but couldn't find any words. Besides, she had always been terrified of Grandmother, with her sharp tongue, cold grey eyes and harsh face. Everyone was terrified of Grandmother, and always had been.

But soon, she thought, there would be nothing left to fear. For Grandmother would be just another shadow . . .

4

An old, withered hand, like a bird's claw, moved across the counterpane, and Grandmother's fingers curled round a black wood box that lay just within reach. 'I have something for you, Lianne,' she said. 'A gift. I want you to keep it always, so whenever you look at it or wear it, you will remember me and say a prayer for my soul.'

Her words sent a cold shiver through Lianne but she tried not to show it. 'Yes Grandmother,' she said again. 'I will.'

'Good. Good.' The lid of the box opened with an unpleasant creaking sound. Grandmother fumbled inside, then drew something out. 'Here, child.'

It was a bracelet. Lianne had seen it before, for it was one of Grandmother's favourites and she always wore it on special occasions. The last such occasion, Lianne remembered, had been the Midsummer banquet in the great hall downstairs. Each year the wealthy families of the district took turns to host the Midsummer feast; this year it had been their turn and there had been rare merriment in Cerne House. Sir Han Carler's son had been very attentive to Gretala that night. Grandmother had disapproved, and the girls had laughed about it afterwards –

The old woman's voice cut across her thoughts. 'Next year, you shall be the one to wear the bracelet. And you will do so in memory of me.'

Startled, Lianne blinked as she realized that Grandmother had read her thoughts. She had always had that uncanny ability. It was frightening . . .

Slowly, she took the bracelet. It was silver, and studded with sapphires. They were cold gems, Lianne thought, as cold as Grandmother, and the idea of wearing them made her shudder inwardly. But she was careful not to let her feelings show as she said, 'Thank you, Grandmother. You are very . . . kind.'

Grandmother had never been kind in her life, but her sunken mouth moved in a sour little smile. 'Go now,' she said.

'And send your sister to me.' She paused. 'You will not see me again, Lianne.'

Lianne was seized with a fear that she would have to kiss Grandmother's wizened cheek, but to her relief the old woman didn't seem to expect it. Nor did Grandmother say goodbye, or give her a blessing; in fact she said nothing more at all, only waved that claw-like hand, dismissing Lianne from the room.

They were all waiting outside: Lord and Lady Cerne, Gretala and Priddy. Gretala went nervously into the bedroom, and though Lianne tried to hear what Grandmother might be saying to her, the only sound that came was the moaning of the wind. Priddy clucked over the sapphire bracelet, but Lord and Lady Cerne showed no interest. They seemed uneasy, as though they were waiting for something unpleasant to happen. And then Gretala emerged.

She was carrying a small, velvet-covered box, and there was a frown on her pretty face. Lady Cerne tensed instantly and would have spoken, but her husband touched her arm.

'No, wife. Not here.' He turned suddenly to the nurse. 'Priddy, take Miss Lianne back to her room.' And, seeing that Lianne was about to object, he added ferociously, '*Now*, woman! Do you hear me?'

Priddy bridled but didn't dare argue. She caught hold of Lianne's arm so hard that her fingers pinched, and replied a little huffily, 'Of course, My Lord. If you say so.'

'But Father –' Lianne began. Priddy shook her and, knowing it was a warning, she fell silent. But she looked back over her shoulder as the nurse hurried her away. Her parents were talking to Gretala, urgently, or so it seemed. Lianne couldn't tell what the conversation was about, but as the wind lulled momentarily one snatch did reach her ears. Her father's voice. And what he said made Lianne's skin crawl.

'*Oh, yes. Oh, yes. This is what I had feared . . .*'

'Now, however should I know what His Lordship wanted to say to your sister?' Priddy closed the shutters of the turret bedroom, then moved to the fire and began to rake the logs with unnecessary vigour. She had her self-righteous look on, and Lianne knew she was still bristling over Lord Cerne's curt dismissal. 'It's not my place to ask.' She looked up. 'And neither is it yours.'

Lianne pouted. 'I only wanted to know what gift Grandmother gave to Gretala. There was no need for Father to speak so harshly.' She sighed, and sat down on her bed. 'But then he always is harsh. He always has been.'

Priddy's face softened a little, for she had been with the family for nearly fifty years and had been nurse to Lord Cerne himself when he was small. 'Not always, Lianne,' she said gently. 'He was different once. A long time ago. But time changes

9

people. And this has never been a happy house.'

As if echoing those last words, the voice of the wind rose suddenly to a doleful wail. The shutters rattled violently and Lianne shivered and hugged herself.

'I wish I could leave, Priddy. I wish I could marry and go away from this house for ever.'

'Now, now,' Priddy chided. 'You're only fifteen; that's too young to think about such things.'

'It isn't too young. Gretala's only two years older, and Mother says she'll probably be betrothed soon.'

'Betrothed's one thing, married's another,' Priddy said, then relented a little. 'Don't fret. Plenty of time for you to find a handsome young man.'

Lianne gave her an odd look. 'Before Cerne House works its dark magic on me, too?'

'Now, I didn't say that.'

'But it's true, isn't it?' Lianne persisted.

'Tezer says there's a curse on this house and everyone in it.'

'Tezer's a fool who should know better than to go spreading rumours,' Priddy retorted. 'And *you*, Miss, shouldn't spend your time in the company of the stable servants! What would your father say if he knew?'

Lianne shrugged. 'He doesn't know. And he won't find out unless you tell him.' She paused. 'But *is* it true, Priddy? About a curse?'

'I'm sure I've no idea.' Priddy's mouth snapped shut so fast and firmly that Lianne knew she was lying. But before Lianne could persevere, the nurse came bustling back to the bed. 'Up from there, now. Your sister will be back at any moment, and then you must both spend an hour at your history.'

'Oh, *Priddy* –'

'A proper lady must be knowledgeable as well as decorative,' said Priddy. 'How can you hope to snare that handsome husband you long for, if you have no learning?'

It was impossible to argue with Priddy's logic when she was in this mood, and Lianne gave in. 'Very well, if I *must*.'

'And put that bracelet away.' Lianne had dropped Grandmother's gift on the bed beside her. 'It isn't respectful just to leave it lying there as it is.'

Lianne frowned. 'I don't like it. I wish Grandmother had chosen to give me something else.'

'Doubtless she had her own good reasons, and it isn't for us to question them. Though I must say that warmer stones would have suited you better. Rubies, maybe. Sapphires are much more your sister's colour, for they match her eyes and set off all that handsome black hair. Now,' Priddy brushed her hands together, making it clear that she was determined to change the subject, 'fetch your books and get ready for your studies. When your sister –'

She stopped, as suddenly a new sound mingled with the wind's wail. The shutters and the turret's thick stone walls muffled it, but they both recognized it instantly. Slowly, mournfully, the great bell that hung in the central tower of Cerne House had begun to toll.

Lianne started to her feet and whispered, '*Grandmother* . . .'

Priddy was listening to the bell and her face had taken on a strange look. At last she spoke. 'Your grandmother is dead.' She shut her eyes. 'Rest her soul.'

And in her voice, Lianne thought, was relief . . . and fear.

Chapter Two

'IT WAS VERY strange.' Gretala's slim, pale fingers stroked the velvet box. 'Grandmother just said that I must keep the necklace and never, ever wear it. And then when I came out of the bedroom, Mother and Father told me to put it away and not even *look* at it again.'

They were sitting together on the floor of their room, in front of the fire. There had been no history studies; the tolling of the bell had stopped all activity as Cerne House went into mourning for Grandmother. Everyone had changed into grey clothes – grey was the colour of death – and the household would fast until a night and a day had passed.

The bell had stopped now that darkness had fallen. But the wind still rampaged, rocking the turret and screaming round the house. Lianne, though, had forgotten her fear of it, and of the shadows. She was too intrigued by Gretala's tale.

'May I see the necklace?' She reached out towards the box.

Gretala looked dubious. 'Father said I wasn't to show it to anyone. Not even you. In fact, especially not you.'

'Why?'

'I don't know,' Gretala said. 'He wouldn't tell me. Mother said that there's a legend about the necklace and it's something to do with that.'

'A legend?' Lianne's green eyes lit eagerly. 'What is it?'

'Mother says I'm too young to understand. She'll tell me when I come of age.'

That struck Lianne as unfair and she

said so, but Gretala only shrugged. Unlike her sister, she knew that there was no point in trying to argue with Lord and Lady Cerne.

Lianne, however, wasn't about to give up. 'At least let me see the necklace!' she pleaded.

'I was told not to.'

'Oh, *please*! No one will ever know. And it can't do any harm if I just look.'

'Well . . .' But Lianne had always been the stronger willed of the two, and Gretala gave way. 'Ohh . . . all right, then. I suppose it can't hurt.'

She opened the velvet box. Inside was a necklace, silver like Lianne's bracelet, and very ornate. But instead of sapphires, a single, huge topaz was set into the centre of the piece.

Lianne breathed out very slowly. The topaz winked in the candlelight, glowing warmly. 'It's *beautiful*,' she said.

Gretala pulled a face. 'Do you think so? I don't like it at all. I think it's . . . I don't know; *creepy*, somehow.' She shivered.

'And knowing that it has a secret makes things worse.'

'Oh, Gretala, you're not afraid of a foolish old legend, are you?' Before her sister could stop her Lianne picked the necklace up. 'I think it's lovely. A hundred times nicer than my bracelet. And besides, if there is a legend about it, why should it be anything dreadful? It's just as likely to be exciting and romantic – like the mirror at Lyndark Hall.'

The Lyndarks were near neighbours. In their great hall hung a mirror, very tiny and so old that the glass had become stained and dim. The story went that any maiden who held a candle to the mirror at midnight would glimpse the face of the man she was destined to marry. Lianne had seen the mirror on a family visit to Lyndark Hall, but to her huge disappointment they hadn't stayed the night and so she had been unable to try it for herself. Now, her romantic imagination stirred anew as she wondered what secrets Gretala's topaz might hold in its strange, glowing depths.

'We could stay awake tonight,' she ventured. 'We could look into the topaz . . .'

Gretala frowned. 'We wouldn't see anything.'

'Oh, we might. Think about it, Gretala – if there *is* a legend, then the topaz must be the key. It's the only jewel in the necklace, after all. And midnight' – she suppressed a little shiver of excitement – 'is always the hour when magic works!'

Gretala wasn't sure that she wanted this or any other magic to work at all. But Lianne was carried away with enthusiasm and, as always, Lianne's enthusiasm was stronger than her sister's timidity.

All the same, Gretala made an effort to draw back. 'But what if we make a mistake?' she said. 'If you're wrong about the legend, we might wake up something *evil.*'

'Oh, you're such a mouse!' Lianne laughed. 'Of course we shan't wake anything evil! I expect nothing will happen at all. It'll just be fun to *try.*' Her mouth curved into a sly smile. 'Wouldn't you *like* to find out who your future husband is? You never know – you might see Valdorne Carler!'

'*Lianne!*' But though Gretala's cheeks had turned pink, she too was beginning to smile. And Lianne knew she had won the battle, just as she always did.

There was no timepiece in the turret room and so they couldn't be sure of the hour. But Lianne had always had an uncanny instinct about midnight. Whatever the season or the weather, somehow she always *knew* when the magic time – the witching-time, as Priddy called it – had arrived. And now, with Cerne House sunk in darkness and silence, she and Gretala lit a single candle and crouched over it, ready to begin.

The gale had gone, but Lianne still felt the echoes of it in her bones. She was keyed up, excited, and the knowledge that what they were doing was secret and forbidden made the excitement all the greater.

Twice, Gretala had almost changed her mind. Lianne had managed to persuade her, but now Gretala didn't want to touch the necklace. So it was Lianne who lifted it out of its box once more and set it on the table, where the candlelight could fall on it.

The topaz seemed to glow with an eerie inner life of its own. It looked like cool fire; or the eye of some unearthly creature, shining in the night. Lianne was captivated. For a moment, as she gazed at the stone, it seemed to call to her, as though it wanted to draw her into its strange, glimmering world . . .

She shook the giddy feeling off and looked at Gretala. 'Now,' she breathed. 'Your turn first. Look into the stone.'

Gretala stared at the topaz. Her body was tense as she concentrated, and Lianne quivered with anticipation. A minute passed, another, and another. Then Gretala shook her head.

'There's nothing there, Lianne. Nothing at all.'

Frustration roiled in Lianne. 'You're giving up too easily! Magic needs time – try again!'

Gretala gazed into the topaz once more. But after another minute or two she sighed and raised her head. 'It's no use. It doesn't work.' She pushed the necklace towards Lianne. 'You try.'

Lianne all but pounced on the necklace. As she bent over it the weird, shivering cry of an owl echoed somewhere out in the night. Gretala jumped and whimpered, but Lianne didn't notice. She was lost in the strange, glowing jewel.

And suddenly, from deep within the jewel, a pair of eyes looked back at her . . .

Lianne's own eyes widened in shock. For one instant she thought that she must be seeing her own reflection in the topaz. But then the other eyes blinked. And now, she could see a face . . .

He was young – only a few years older than herself. He had high cheekbones, a fine yet strong jaw, and a mouth which, Lianne knew in her soul, could smile the most beautiful smile in the entire world. But that mouth wasn't smiling. Instead, it was twisted in a bitter and terrible look. A look of rage – and of such pain that Lianne felt emotion catch violently in her throat.

She made a breathless, gasping sound and heard Gretala hiss, 'What is it? What can you see?' But she could pay no heed to Gretala. The boy's eyes – dark eyes, *angry* eyes – were locked with her own, and in them was a plea, a yearning –

'Lianne!' Gretala's hand caught her by the shoulder. 'What is it? Tell me!'

Lianne could barely breathe. '*Look!*' she whispered. '*Look – can you see him?*'

She felt Gretala move nearer. 'I can't –' Gretala began. Then suddenly: '*Ohh . . .*'

But as Gretala bent closer, the eyes of the boy in the jewel widened. The yearning look vanished, and fear took its place.

Instinct told Lianne what would happen, and she cried out, 'No, wait! *Please –*'

But it was too late. He was already

turning, retreating. Lianne saw the flicker of long hair, dark as a raven's wing, and the swirl of a cloak. Then without any warning the candle guttered and went out, plunging the turret room – and the topaz – into darkness.

Gretala screamed and jumped back. 'Oh, Lianne! The candle!'

'We've got to light it again!' Lianne groped frantically for the tinder-box, which she *knew* she had left on the table. She found it, scrabbled to get a spark . . . The candle flared into life once more and she saw Gretala sitting wide-eyed on the floor, one hand clamped over her mouth.

But Lianne wasn't interested in her sister. She snatched up the necklace and peered into the jewel, desperately, *desperately* willing the strange, beautiful boy still to be there.

The stone glowed back at her. The image was gone.

'I don't care.' Gretala hugged her knees under the bedcovers. She was still shaking.

'I don't care who he is or why you saw him. I think it's *dangerous*. And I don't *ever* want to look at that necklace again!'

Lianne wasn't in bed yet. She had lit three more candles and sat at her dressing-table, brushing the long tresses of her hair. Hair which, she realized now, was almost the same colour as the topaz.

'I do,' she said. Her eyes had a far-away look as she remembered the face in the jewel. So angry, yet so sad. And so beautiful . . . 'I want to see him again,' she went on dreamily. 'I want to find out who he is. I want to know *everything* about him.'

'Oh, Lianne!' Gretala protested. 'There's nothing *to* know. He wasn't real. We just imagined it, that was all!'

'We can't both have imagined exactly the same thing.' Then Lianne gave her sister a sidelong look. 'And anyway, if you think he isn't real, why are you so frightened?'

Gretala opened her mouth, but shut it again as she realized Lianne had trapped her. 'Well, whether he is or isn't,' she said defensively, 'I wish Grandmother had never given me that necklace! I don't want to have to look after it. I don't want it anywhere near me at all, ever again!'

For a long moment Lianne stared at her. 'Then why don't we exchange our gifts?'

'*What?*'

'Why not? You hate the necklace; I don't like my bracelet.'

'But the bracelet's lovely!'

'Well then, it's simple, isn't it? Priddy says sapphires suit you much better anyway. If you like the bracelet, you have it – and I'll have the necklace.'

Gretala shook her head, though Lianne could see she was tempted. 'We couldn't! Father and Mother would be furious!'

'We needn't tell them, you goose! We needn't tell anyone. The necklace is supposed to be kept out of sight anyway. And if you want to wear the bracelet, we can pretend I've lent it to you.'

Gretala bit her lip. 'Well . . .'

Whenever Gretala said 'Well . . .' in that

way, Lianne knew she had won. She sprang from her chair, snatched up the sapphire bracelet and ran to her sister. 'Look at the bracelet, Gretala. Try it on!' She fastened the catch around the slim wrist. 'It's perfect for you! Now, give me the necklace and I'll put it safely away.'

Slowly, Gretala picked up the velvet box and handed it over. But her blue eyes were full of doubt.

'You will be careful, won't you, Lianne? You won't do anything . . . foolish?'

'Of course I won't!' Lianne's heart was leaping, singing with excitement as she clutched the box to her breast.

'And you *promise* never to tell anyone?'

'I promise.' Lianne licked her finger and touched it to her sister's brow. '*By briar and thorn may I be torn, if e'er I break this vow I make,*' she intoned solemnly. 'There, now. Is that good enough?'

Gretala shivered at the grim old promise-rhyme, but she was reassured. She watched as Lianne climbed into her own bed. One by one they snuffed out the candles, and the darkness of the night closed in on them.

'I hope I don't dream about that strange boy tonight,' Gretala said.

Lianne stared into the dark. The necklace in its case was under her pillow. Gretala hadn't seen her put it there; she thought it was safely hidden.

So softly that her sister couldn't hear, Lianne whispered, *'You won't dream about him, Gretala. But I will. I know I will.'*

Chapter Three

GRANDMOTHER'S FUNERAL took place two days later. The procession left Cerne House at sunset, winding its way from the great front door, along the drive and on towards the Grove of the Dead. The Grove was about half a mile from the house – a circle of tall poplar trees with an avenue of dark and brooding yews leading up to it. There, Grandmother would be laid to rest among the Cerne ancestors, and soon there would be a new stone carving in the Grove to commemorate her.

Gloomy dusk was closing in as the cortège neared the Grove. First came the coffin itself, on a bier carried by four hooded men and covered by wreaths of yew and ivy. The Cerne family walked behind the bier, with the servants following them. The Cernes wore grey cloaks with hoods drawn over their faces, and all were veiled. This was an old and grim tradition, for Death would be present in the Grove tonight, and if he should see the faces of Grandmother's family, he might reach out for them too. Everyone carried a lit candle, and the line of sombre figures moving through the twilight with their tiny flames made an eerie sight. The wind still moaned, as it had done for days, and tonight it sounded lost and bitter.

Lianne walked beside Gretala. She held her candle solemnly before her and murmured her prayers as she must, but her mind wasn't on Grandmother. Instead, she looked through her veil at the groups of people who waited beside the track to pay their last respects. It seemed that nearly everyone in the district had come. Their neighbours, all Lord Cerne's tenants. There was even a small company of witch-women, who made magical blessing-signs and set up their strange, wailing lament as the cortège passed. The sound of their voices mingling with the wind made Lianne shiver.

They reached the Grove and the candles bobbed like will-o'-the-wisps along the yew avenue. Among the murky shadows of the poplar trees the priest and his attendants were waiting, and people gathered round to listen silently as the rites began.

Lianne had been to a funeral only once before, and had had bad dreams about it for weeks afterwards. Funerals were *frightening*. The dismal words of the rite chilled her blood, and the dull, dead ringing of the attendants' handbells made goose-flesh break out on her skin. Her candle kept guttering, too, and she was afraid it might go out. That would be horrifying, for the little flames were said to give protection from the evil spirits which haunted the Grove. And she *hated* the hood's muffling folds and the way the veil blurred everything. It all felt very nightmarish, and nervously Lianne prayed that the rite would soon be over.

To distract herself she dared to turn her head a little and peeked at the watchers now gathered at the edge of the Grove. One woman seemed to be crying, which, remembering Grandmother, Lianne thought was strange. One man kept making religious signs in the air, as if he were frightened. And further away, between two trees, someone else was standing apart from the crowd. Where had he come from? The procession hadn't passed him on the track. In fact only a minute ago he hadn't been there at all . . .

Suddenly Lianne's heart seemed to jump and tighten inside her. There was something *familiar* about that solitary figure. She couldn't see his face with the veil and the gloom to hamper her, but she was certain he wasn't anyone from the district. Yet she *knew* him. She *did* . . .

Gretala nudged her, and Lianne realized she had been staring off into the distance, oblivious to the ceremony. Luckily Lord and Lady Cerne hadn't noticed, and Lianne quickly turned her attention back to the prayers she was supposed to be repeating. But her gaze kept wandering back to the solitary figure. Each time she looked, he was still there. And she had an eerie certainty that he was watching her.

Then suddenly he moved. Lianne saw him flit like a ghost between the trees, the wind catching his black hair and the edge of his cloak. For a few moments she lost sight of him as he vanished behind a group of mourners, but then he appeared again, closer to where she stood.

And Lianne's green eyes widened in shock as, for the first time, she saw his face. *He was the boy in the topaz! The beautiful, bitter and sad boy who had gazed back at her from the depths of the jewel!*

Lianne made a choking noise which she quickly turned into a cough as Gretala turned to look at her in surprise. Awe and excitement and bewilderment filled Lianne, and she stared in astonishment at the stranger, hardly able to believe what her eyes were telling her. But there could be no mistake. He *was* the boy in the jewel. And all Lianne's fancies about the topaz and its legend sprang abruptly back into life. This was no mere chance – this was Fate. It *had* to be! She had seen his face in the gem, and now he was here, as real as she. Like the Lyndark mirror, the topaz necklace had shown her her destiny!

The funeral rites were drawing towards their close. In a few minutes the priest would lead them in the doleful elegy-song, then Grandmother's coffin would be lowered into the earth. Lianne's candle-flame was trembling as her hands shook. She could barely contain her impatience, and she dreaded that the boy might leave the Grove before the ceremony ended. For she believed that when she saw his face in

33

the jewel, he had also seen hers, perhaps in a dream or vision. Now though, veiled as she was, he couldn't possibly recognize her. And the thought that he might go away without ever knowing how close they had come to each other was more than Lianne could bear.

The elegy-song began, and somehow she forced herself to concentrate enough to sing with the others. The coffin was lowered to the bells' melancholy accompaniment, and the priest pronounced a blessing and protection-wish on all. At last then the ceremony was over, and sighs of relief whispered audibly round the Grove as people began to depart.

Lord Cerne beckoned his daughters and turned towards the yew avenue. As they emerged from the Grove, Lianne suddenly felt a lurch of dismay. The black-haired boy was no longer there! He had gone, disappeared! Wildly she looked around, but there were people everywhere, and in the dark it was impossible to tell one shape from another.

Then she saw him. He was halfway along the avenue, standing alone under one of the spreading yew trees. Quite how she could be so certain that it *was* him, Lianne didn't know; but she was. Her heart began to thump as though it were trying to break out through her ribs, and silently she pleaded, *Oh please, don't go! Don't go before I can get closer!* For a wild idea had come to her. Her father might be furious, her mother outraged, but she didn't care. They weren't in the Grove now; Death wouldn't stretch out a bony hand to grasp hold of her. She *had* to let the strange boy see her face!

They were moving on down the avenue. Closer, Lianne thought; just a little closer . . . They were almost level with the boy now. He hadn't moved. He was still watching. The Cernes walked past him – and quickly, before her nerve could fail her, Lianne raised her hands. Her veil swept aside, her hood fell back. And as her face in its frame of vivid auburn hair was revealed, she turned and looked boldly and directly at the stranger.

In that same instant the moon came out from behind a cloud, and for one moment, just one, they saw each other clearly. The boy's dark eyes widened – then suddenly, before Lianne could make any further move, he turned with a whirl of cloak and flick of hair, and was gone.

'Lianne!' Gretala caught hold of her sister's arm. 'Lianne, what are you *doing*? Raise your hood, before Father notices!'

Lianne shook her off, but replaced the hood and veil. They didn't matter now. That one moment had allowed her to see the stranger plainly enough to banish any last doubts. He *was* the boy in the topaz. Her fate. Her destiny. She knew he was real now, for she had seen him in the flesh. And he in turn had seen her, and knew at last who she was.

Lianne looked back over her shoulder several times as the family walked on. But the figure among the yews did not reappear, and intuition told her that this time he was truly gone. No matter. Some unearthly magic had drawn him close to her tonight, and that magic was not done with her yet. She would see him again. He would return. He must. He *must*.

Chapter Four

IN THE DEEP of the night, Lianne woke from a strange dream. In the dream she had been gazing into the topaz again, hoping and praying that she would see the black-haired boy's face. But he did not appear. Instead, she seemed to hear a voice echoing in her mind; a voice that called her name over and over again. Then suddenly the dream vanished and she found herself awake in the turret room.

The moon was covered by cloud again and it was very dark. Lianne could hear Gretala breathing in the other bed but couldn't see her. She pulled up her blankets and was about to snuggle back under them when something made her pause. A faint sound . . . or had she imagined it? Lianne lay very still, listening. The old house creaked at night, but that wasn't what she had heard. Nor was it the wind. Something else . . .

Then the hairs on the back of her neck stood up as a voice drifted faintly and spectrally through the window.

'*Lianne . . . Lianne . . .*'

Lianne shot bolt upright in bed, staring into the dark. No, her mind said, no! It wasn't possible! It must have been the voice of the wind in the trees!

'*Lianne . . . I'm here, Lianne . . .*'

A wave of heat followed by a wave of icy cold went through Lianne. It was *his* voice! Somewhere deep down, a part of her mind tried to argue that she couldn't possibly know that, but she ignored it. She *did* know, and suddenly she found herself out of bed. There was a candle at the bedside; she snatched it up and lit it, then padded quickly, barefoot, towards the door. The latch squeaked but Gretala didn't stir, and Lianne slipped out of the room and began to tiptoe down the spiral stairs.

If she had stopped to think, she would have been horrified by the thought of creeping about the house alone in the dark. But somehow it didn't occur to her to feel afraid. Another kind of power had her in its grip, and she couldn't resist it. She *had* to answer the call of that voice!

Down the stairs and along the landing Lianne went, her candle casting shadows that loomed menacingly at her. Cold draughts nibbled at her ankles, and by the time she reached the house's ground floor she was shivering. But she couldn't turn back. On through the hall, then into the cavernous kitchen, empty and echoey now. And beyond the kitchen, the door to the garden. Her bedroom window overlooked the garden, and that was where the voice had come from.

The bolts of the door were heavy and

stiff, but Lianne wrestled with them until they drew back with a clank. Hand on the latch, she paused for a moment . . . then eagerness overcame her fear, and she pulled the door open.

The moon had appeared again, and the garden was a patchwork of chilly silver light and ominous black shadows. But there was no one there. Just empty lawns and terraces, and the bizarre shapes of the clipped hedges. Lianne stared dazedly at the scene – then jumped like a startled cat as a mournful, hooting call quivered out of the night.

The owl swooped from the tree and floated across the lawn like a grey phantom. As it passed it cried again, and the sound seemed to become a word: '*Lianne* . . .' Then it was gone – and as it disappeared, Lianne's senses came down to earth with a violent jolt. What was she *doing* here? This was insane! There was no one calling to her. Only an owl. And she was alone in the dark house, in the dead of night, among the shadows . . .

She shut the door so fast that it almost rebounded from the jamb. Scrabble with the bolts, mustn't leave any clues – *Oh, candle, don't go out, please!* Then away, back through the kitchen to the hall, to the stairs, hunching and scurrying like a frightened little animal. Her courage had vanished in the space of an instant, as if it had been part of her dream. Perhaps it *had* been a dream. Perhaps she had walked in her sleep and only come to when confronted by the garden and the cold night air. But she was wide awake now, and frightened of the shadows and the ghosts they might contain.

If there were ghosts in the shadows, however, they did not touch Lianne. She reached the turret room safely and collapsed on her bed, gasping. Gretala was still asleep, and after a few minutes Lianne climbed under the blankets and pulled them up to her chin. She felt better now, and Gretala's presence was reassuring. She had just been silly, that was all. There had been nothing to be afraid of.

But it was a long time before she dared blow the candle out.

Lianne seemed to be in a world of her own the next day. She was silent at breakfast, and during morning lessons was twice in trouble with her dry and dusty old tutor for not attending. Priddy, in a rare cross moment, declared that Lianne wasn't listening to a single word anyone said and that she washed her hands of the child. Even Gretala couldn't get through the secretive wall that Lianne had built around herself.

Privately, though, Lianne was thinking very hard indeed. She still couldn't decide whether her strange experience had been real. Had someone been calling to her in the night, or had she merely had a dream and walked in her sleep? It was a puzzle that she couldn't answer, and it nagged at her. Tonight, she resolved, she would do her best to stay awake, and see what happened.

Lianne was so willing – almost eager, in

fact – to go to bed early that Priddy was faintly suspicious. However, she said nothing, only made a mental note to watch the girl tomorrow in case she should be sickening for something.

But Lianne's plan didn't work out as she had hoped. With her rest broken on the previous night she was very tired, and by the time Gretala came up to the turret room she had fallen fast asleep. She did dream, but only about arguing with her tutor. She was just reaching the point where the old scholar was threatening to report her to Lord Cerne, who would punish her for impudence, when abruptly she woke.

Tonight, there was moonlight filtering in at the latticed window; enough for Lianne to make out her sister's form in the other bed. She sat up carefully, peering about her and trying to remember where she had left the candle in its stand . . . and then froze as she heard a soft whisper from outside.

'*Lianne . . .*'

Lianne swallowed hard, then pinched herself. Nothing happened; the room didn't dissolve around her as she had half expected it to. She wasn't asleep, then, and this wasn't a dream. The voice *was* real. And as she listened, it came again.

'*Lianne . . . look down, Lianne. I'm here.*'

Lianne was out of bed like a cat bolting from a cage. She ran to the window (oh, if only she dared open it! But Gretala might wake) and peered out into the night.

The wind was still muttering and gusting around the eaves of the house, and the swaying branches of nearby trees cast confusing shadows across the garden. For a moment Lianne saw only the still, dark hedges, the cold, moonlit stone of the terrace. But then . . .

Her breath caught quickly in her throat. For on the lawn beyond the terrace, motionless, was a human figure. From this distance Lianne could make out no detail; his face was only a pale and featureless blur in the darkness. But he wore a cloak. And his hair was black.

'*Ohhh . . .*' The sound escaped her before she could stop it. It was a small sound, very soft, and Gretala didn't stir. But the figure on the lawn did. As though he had heard her, he raised a hand and beckoned. And the eerie voice reached Lianne again: 'I *am here, Lianne. I am here.*'

Lianne grabbed the candle and lit it, her fingers trembling so much that she almost burned herself. Then she flew out of the room, down the stairs and away towards the kitchen. Wild thoughts rushed through her mind, blotting out her terror of the dark. Last night *had* been real! But she hadn't been quick enough; he must have gone before she could reach the garden. This time, she thought, she *must* catch up with him, and as she ran she whispered a breathless plea: '*Oh, please, wait for me! Don't go before I can reach you!*'

She stumbled into the kitchen, raced to the door. Those wretched stiff bolts! But at last they thumped back and Lianne flung the door open.

And he was there. He was waiting for her. She saw him by the ornamental pool where no one sat any more because there were no longer any fish to watch, and as the moonlight fell on his face she felt her heart miss a painful beat. It *was* him. It *was*. The boy in the topaz. The boy who had come to Grandmother's funeral. And, unbidden, the heady thought swept through Lianne's mind: *My own . . . my beloved . . .*

Her heart was pounding now, like a hammer inside her. She took a step forward, hesitantly, and one hand started to reach out.

'Who are you?' she whispered wonderingly.

The black-haired boy's head came up sharply. For a single moment Lianne saw him very clearly as her gaze met his. Then, so fast that she couldn't react, he turned and strode away across the garden.

Dismay stabbed through Lianne and she cried, 'No! Wait, don't go!' But he took no notice, only quickened his pace.

And suddenly something in Lianne seemed to snap. She hitched up the skirt of her long nightgown, and before she knew what she was doing she had started after him.

'Wait!' she called again. 'Wait, please!'

But he only moved faster. Now he was almost running – or, strangely, *gliding* – across the grass. Lianne redoubled her efforts, not caring about the cold or the wet grass under her feet, only desperate to catch up with him, not to let him elude her yet again. On she ran – but however fast she went, he seemed to draw further and further away. She saw him pass through the big iron gate at the end of the garden and she stumbled out after him. Before her now was the rutted track that led to the woods and, beyond them, the moorland. He was already halfway along the track, heading for the trees, and a heavy mist was coming down, obscuring him from her sight. She mustn't lose him, Lianne thought frantically, she *mustn't*! But though she called and cried, he wouldn't stop. And now he had reached the trees and was disappearing into the darkness of the wood–

Lianne raced into the wood. Tree-trunks rushed past her in a blur – then suddenly she slithered to a halt, gasping for breath. He was gone. He had vanished without trace, and though she strained her ears to listen she couldn't even hear the sound of his feet in the undergrowth.

Tears started into her eyes. Which way had he *gone*? There were so many paths through the wood, so many directions he might have taken. Where *was* he? And why, oh *why* had he run away from her? He had come to the house to find her. He knew her name. He had *called* her. Yet as soon as she answered his call, he had run away. It didn't make any *sense*.

Lianne wiped her eyes fiercely, then, as her blurred vision cleared, she began to feel frightened. The wood was so dark; dark and horribly silent. The bare trees looked like tangled bones, grim and menacing, and she had a hideous feeling that at any moment they could take on a life of their own and close in around her like a cage. She started to shiver uncontrollably, and a frightened little moan came from her lips. The lonely terrors of the night were far worse than any of the shadows that lurked in Cerne House. And he, her beloved – for she was certain now that that was what he was – was not here, and she didn't have the courage to try to find him.

The tears were trying to start again; tears of fear and misery and confusion. Lianne bit them back, then turned and ran, away from the wood, away from the darkness, towards the safety of home.

Chapter Five

LIANNE FOUND HER way safely back to Cerne House. It was a nerve-racking journey, but nothing pursued her from the wood as she had feared, nor did she lose her way in the thickening mist. To her huge relief she was able to slip back into the house and up to the turret room without anyone being the wiser. And when finally she went to sleep, her mind was working on the bones of a plan.

By the following evening she had made her resolution: if the handsome boy from the topaz returned again tonight – and Lianne believed he would – then she would *really* be ready. She would be waiting for him. Not in the turret but in the garden. It should be easy enough for her to sneak out once the household was asleep; after all, hadn't she already done it twice? And when he appeared this time, he wouldn't elude her. She wouldn't *let* him.

She was so quiet that day that when bedtime came Priddy insisted on giving her a tonic drink. Lianne didn't like it but submitted meekly, and soon afterwards she dutifully kissed her parents good-night and went up to the turret. When Gretala came in she pretended to be asleep, making sure that the covers were pulled up around her chin so that Gretala wouldn't see she was still fully dressed. And as soon as the house was silent, Lianne slipped out of bed, picked up her cloak and outdoor shoes and crept downstairs.

The night was very still. For the first

time in many days the wind had dropped, and the mist Lianne had encountered last night was now curling and creeping around the house. The garden looked like a strange, unearthly white lake, the clipped hedges floating on its surface. Somewhere, a long way off, a dog was barking and the noise echoed eerily. Lianne had left a lantern ready in the scullery; she picked it up, closed the garden door carefully behind her and walked towards the pool. This was where she had seen him last night; this was surely where she would find him again. On a stone seat, hidden by a tall and overgrown bush, she lit her lantern and sat down to wait.

Time seemed to pass very slowly, and once Lianne almost fell asleep despite the cold. But at last she was alerted by a sound close by. Her pulse quickened and, very cautiously, she peered around the bush.

He was approaching from the direction of the garden's north gate. She couldn't see his face in the mist, only his dark cloak and the even darker hair above it. But it was him.

He stopped by the pool and stood gazing towards the turret window. Lianne took a deep breath, raised her lantern and stepped out from behind the bush. The boy's head turned swiftly – and then, just as he had done last night, he turned and ran.

This time, though, Lianne was ready. She had expected this, expected him to flee again, and she didn't even pause to call after him but took off on his heels, racing with all the speed she could summon. He was a swift runner but this time he didn't have such an advantage, and by the time Lianne ran through the gate and on to the woodland track he was only a short way ahead of her. Again, strangely, he seemed to *glide* over the ground, his feet almost skimming, and she realized suddenly that she couldn't hear the thud of his footsteps. Was he a ghost? She didn't know – but at this moment she didn't care.

The boy reached the wood, his cloak and hair flying behind him like a great, dark wing. And Lianne, her lantern swinging wildly, sprinted after him, determined not to let him out of her sight. She didn't have breath for calling out, but inside she was shouting silently, '*No, wait, I won't let you go this time!*' In a curious way it was as if the boy knew what she was thinking, for when he reached a fork in the path he paused and looked back, as if to be sure that she was still following. Lianne's pounding heart lurched with hope and she raced on. Through the wood, between the trees, branches whipping in her face and scratching her, roots tangling her feet and trying to trip her up. Once she did trip, and sprawled full-length in a carpet of dead leaves. But she was up in an instant and running once more, straining to keep the boy's fleeing figure in sight.

She burst out of the wood so unexpectedly that the shock made her flounder to a halt. One moment she was fighting her way among looming tree-trunks; the next they were gone and the moor lay ahead of her. Lianne stood still, struggling to get her breath back, and stared at the ominous landscape stretching away into darkness and mist. She didn't like the moor, for it was a bleak and empty and lonely place, and Priddy told gruesome stories about *things* that haunted it at the dead of night. But although Priddy's tales frightened her, more frightening still was the thought of losing sight of the boy. She could still see him dimly in the mist, and with a tremendous effort she screwed up her courage and started after him again.

So began a nerve-racking and uncanny journey as Lianne pursued her quarry across the moor. Sometimes she thought he had vanished for good, but then she would glimpse him again and the chase would begin once more. It was clear that he didn't want to escape altogether, yet at the same time he wasn't about to let her catch up with him. At least, not yet . . . for now Lianne was certain that he was deliberately leading her somewhere. Where he was going, and what would happen when they reached his destination, she couldn't begin to imagine. But she felt sure he was taking her closer to the heart of this mystery.

And then, to her horror, she really did lose him. How it happened she didn't know, but he simply – *vanished*. And when she waited, thinking he would reappear as he had done before, there was no further sign of him.

Lianne began to shake with fear. The mist was so dense now that her lantern was all but useless, and she felt as though she were suddenly lost in huge, grey, silent emptiness. Where was he? Where had he *gone*? Oh no, she thought; oh no, no –

'*Lianne.*'

The voice came softly out of the gloom, from somewhere quite close by. Her heart crashing under her ribs, Lianne turned and tried to follow its direction. Two steps, three, four – and something loomed ahead of her. She gave a startled cry and almost dropped the lantern before she realized that it was nothing more sinister than a wall, with a jagged edge where old stones had crumbled away. A ruined house . . . Curiosity filled her, for Priddy's stories had never made any mention of ruins out here. But the moor, it seemed, had more secrets than even Priddy knew . . .

Slowly, Lianne started to walk towards the ruin. As she drew closer she could see that once, long ago, a fine house had stood here; perhaps as fine as Cerne. But its wealth and grandeur were long gone. All that remained now were broken and blackened stones, gaping windows and a flight of sweeping steps that led to nothing but brambles.

She climbed up the steps and, reaching the top, peered at the dark undergrowth beyond. Where *was* the boy? She had been certain that the call came from this direction. But there was no sign of anyone . . .

Then, behind her, a foot slid on stone.

Lianne gave a little cry, spun round – and came face to face with the boy. He was gazing at her, his expression grave, and her heart seemed to stop, twist within her and then start beating again ten times more rapidly. Wildly, she thought, *There's something about him that frightens me! Yet . . . yet I'm certain he doesn't mean me any harm. And he looks so sad . . .*

Then the thought collapsed as the boy raised his hands and laid them, very gently, on her shoulders. A thrilling tingle went through Lianne – he was no ghost! His touch was real; she could feel the warmth of his fingers through her cloak. Breath catching in her throat, she whispered, 'Who *are* you?'

The boy's dark eyes continued to gaze steadily into hers. 'My name', he said, 'is Renard.'

'Renard?' She had never heard such a name before, and yet, strangely, something about it seemed familiar. Uncertainly Lianne reached up and touched his cheek. 'Where are you from?' she asked. 'Where do you live? And how do you know who I am?'

His eyelashes came down, masking his expression. 'I know who you are because you called to me.'

'I called to you . . .?'

'Through the topaz. When you looked into the jewel, we saw each other. You called to me, and I had to answer.'

Lianne gasped. Then the necklace truly *was* a magic legacy . . . and, somehow, she had woken the magic to life.

Yet now that she was face to face with the boy at last, she was beginning to feel afraid. 'Play with fire', Priddy always warned, 'and you'll burn your fingers.' What was this, if not fire? This power that had called a stranger from . . . from where? She didn't know where Renard had come from. She didn't know who he was. Or even – and this was the worst thought of all – *what* he was.

He seemed to know what was in her mind. 'I'm not a sprite or a genie that came from the topaz, Lianne. Nor a demon. I promise I'm as human as you are.'

Lianne desperately wanted to believe him. But dared she? 'You said you *had* to answer,' she challenged. 'Why? Why did you *have* to?'

'Because you're the girl I have been waiting for all my life.'

Lianne was stunned. For as he spoke the words, an answering emotion had shivered through her. *The girl I have been waiting for all my life* . . . She believed him. It was absurd, it was mad, but she *believed* him. And though she didn't understand why, and not understanding was frightening, her own feelings were rising like a tide . . .

She gazed back at Renard. His handsome face was so young, and yet there was something about him that seemed far, far older. As though he had lived through bitter troubles and learned hard lessons. That sadness in his dark eyes; a far-away, yearning look that seemed to speak silently of some terrible but deeply private tragedy. But now the yearning was focused upon her . . .

'Lianne . . .' He raised one hand from her shoulder, and his fingers caught hers where they trembled against his cheek. Despite her fear, Lianne felt the sense of magic and wonder fill her again at his touch. Then his hair brushed her face, soft, like fine silk or velvet. She knew what was about to happen and a part of her tried to say, *No, this is wrong! I don't know him, I shouldn't be here, we shouldn't be alone together!* But her heart and soul refused to listen. All that mattered in the world was that Renard was stooping to kiss her, and when his lips touched hers it was like fire and ice and sunlight. They stayed very still, Lianne neither wanting nor daring to move for fear that the enchantment would shatter and leave her lost and alone. Then at last, gently, the kiss ended – and suddenly reality came back like the cold autumn wind. Tears started in Lianne's eyes and, her voice almost breaking, she said, 'Oh, Renard . . . what am I doing?

We're strangers, we don't even know each other!'

'No, Lianne, we're not strangers.' He stroked her hair. 'You saw me in the jewel and you called out. And in your heart I believe you know why you called – and why I answered.'

He was right. In her heart, as he said, Lianne knew the truth more surely than she had ever known anything in her life. But she couldn't make herself confess it. She couldn't say, *It was because I love you.* Not because she didn't want to – she did; oh, she *did*! – but because she didn't dare. So many times in romantic day-dreams she had imagined what it would be like to whisper those words and mean them. But now, at the very moment when the dream had come true, her courage failed. For this wonderful, magical thing was happening too swiftly and too powerfully. She was overwhelmed by the night, by her emotions, by Renard.

Anguished, she started to say helplessly, 'I can't –'

'Hush.' Renard kissed her again, on the brow this time. 'Don't be afraid. I've found you now and I won't let you go again.' He turned her face up towards his and she saw that he was smiling a wistful smile. 'Only follow your heart. That's all I ask of you.'

Lianne started to cry. She didn't know why the tears came; perhaps it was the touch of his hand so warm against her cheek, or perhaps just the chill of the night.

Or perhaps it was the ache that made her feel as though something inside her was breaking apart . . .

It was too much for her, and fear flared like a torch as she tried to pull away from him.

'I must go home!' she cried. 'I can't stay.' She looked at him, appealing to him. 'Please understand – I *daren't* stay!'

'Hush,' Renard said again. He drew her against him and his arms slipped around her, holding her close. A scent clung about him, wood-smoke and sweetbriar and something elusive that she couldn't name.

Renard whispered, 'There's time for us, Lianne. All the time in the world. I've waited so long for you, I can wait a little longer.'

Lianne felt a surge of desperate relief, for above all she needed time. Time to recover, to think, to try to understand. And yet . . . in her heart, if she only dared admit it, she knew that she had no doubts. Renard had been waiting for her. And she, in her turn, had been waiting for him.

She stepped back a pace, still holding his hands but putting a small distance between them. 'Oh, Renard,' she said tremulously, 'I do so want to see you again.'

He smiled. 'You only have to call, and I'll answer.'

'Then . . . tomorrow.' Her pulse was pounding. 'I'll come back tomorrow. At midnight.'

'I'll wait for you. At the edge of the wood, where the track begins.'

'You could come to the house –'

'No.' He said it so quickly that she was taken aback. 'No, I won't come to Cerne again unless I must.'

'Why?' Lianne didn't understand. But Renard only shook his head.

'There are reasons. I can't explain. Please, Lianne, trust me. One day, I promise, I will tell you – but not yet.'

Lianne nodded slowly. 'I trust you.' And she did. She trusted Renard as she would trust no one else in the world.

Her hands clasped his tightly for a moment. Then, with a great effort, she made herself break free.

'I must go home. If anyone should find me gone –'

'I'll see you safely back to the garden gate. And tomorrow –'

'I'll be there. I promise, Renard.' Her heart was like a butterfly caged inside her, beating its wings, striving to get free. 'I *promise*.'

Chapter Six

LIANNE, *YOU CAN'T*!' Gretala stared at her sister in horror. 'You don't know anything about him – it could be *dangerous*!'

Lianne shook her head stubbornly. 'It isn't dangerous, Gretala.'

'You can't possibly know that,' Gretala insisted. 'All he's told you about himself is his name. Where does he live? Who are his family? He won't answer those questions. Oh, Lianne, this is something strange, and it scares me!'

'Well, you don't have to get involved if

you don't want to,' Lianne retorted. She was growing annoyed with Gretala, and very disappointed. She had so looked forward to telling her secret and had been sure that Gretala would share the romantic excitement of her adventure. But it seemed that Gretala could see only peril and risk.

'I thought you'd at least *try* to understand,' she went on resentfully. 'After all, you were with me when I looked into the topaz, and –'

Gretala interrupted. 'But that's why I'm frightened, don't you see?' She glanced uneasily around. They were in the drawing room, where they were supposed to be sewing, but their work and needle-boxes lay abandoned. Outside it was raining, and the rain made pattering sounds on the window like ghostly fingers tapping. Gretala shivered. 'This is some kind of bewitchment, Lianne. I don't know what you did when you looked into the jewel, but I wish you hadn't been so reckless! You've conjured something up! Something that should have been left alone!'

'Oh, nonsense!' Lianne pushed away a niggling little doubt and frowned angrily at her sister. 'I said the other day that you're a mouse, Gretala, and you are! I'm not bewitched!'

'But it's *magic* –'

'Of course it's magic! But it's no more sinister than the Lyndark mirror. In fact I think it's just like the mirror, only more powerful. In the mirror you only *see* your true love, but the topaz can *call* him. And it called Renard to me!'

Gretala bit her lip. In truth she was enraptured by Lianne's story, and more than a little envious, for nothing so exciting had ever happened to her except in daydreams. But she had a very uneasy feeling about this. She sensed danger. And even if she was just being a mouse, as Lianne said, she couldn't shake the feeling off.

She made one last effort. 'Lianne, you can't go and meet him again. Not at night. It's too great a risk!'

'It isn't a risk at all,' Lianne said firmly. 'I trust Renard.'

'But Father and Mother –'

'They won't know, unless you tell them.' Lianne's eyes narrowed and became fierce. 'And you won't tell them, will you?'

'I ought to,' Gretala argued unhappily, 'for your sake.'

'*No!*' Lianne sprang to her feet and grabbed her sister's arm. 'You won't, Gretala! Promise me!'

'You're hurting!'

'*Promise!*' Lianne repeated furiously. 'Because if you do tell, then Father will know you gave me the necklace, won't he? And you weren't even supposed to show it to me. You were supposed to put it away and never look at it. What do you think Father will say to that?'

Gretala looked frightened. 'He mustn't find out . . .'

'Then you won't tell him, will you? Or Mother, or Priddy, or anyone. Promise! By briar and thorn!'

Gretala gave in. She repeated the

promise-rhyme, adding, 'But oh, Lianne, if anything terrible should happen to you –'

'It won't.' Lianne had her promise now and was satisfied. She smiled. 'Don't worry, Gretala. This is magic, but it's *good* magic. I won't come to any harm.'

For all Gretala's fears, Lianne was right. And by the end of her second tryst with Renard, the thing she had both longed for and dreaded had happened. She was deeply and helplessly in love.

She returned from the ruined house that night with the memory of Renard's kisses like a flame in her mind. And from then on, every moment of her life was filled with thoughts of the strange, dark boy. By day his face haunted her mind, and when she slept he walked beside her in her dreams. The doubts and fears she had felt at their first meeting were gone, and in her heart now she knew that he was the one – the only one – for her.

They began to meet every night. Always

Renard would wait for Lianne by the woodland track, and always they went back to the ruin on the moor. Lianne grew to love the ruin, for it was a secret and private place where no one could disturb them. She felt that it was their very own. And in its strange way it seemed more like a true home to her than Cerne House with its gloom and shadows had ever done. She was happy at the ruin. Happy with Renard. And her happiness was made all the greater by the knowledge that Renard returned her love in full measure.

But for all the joy and fulfilment of their trysts, there was one cloud in Lianne's sky. She was certain now that she and Renard were destined to be together, yet still she knew nothing about him. Time after time she had begged him to explain, but Renard only shook his head gently and sadly. 'One day, I promise I will tell you everything,' he would say. 'But not yet. Please, trust me in this, and try to be patient.'

Lianne did try. But it was hard; so hard

for her that at last, one chill, windswept night as they stood together in the shelter of the broken wall, she couldn't bear it any longer. When she asked her question yet again, and yet again Renard would not answer, she caught his hands in a desperate clasp.

'*Why* can't you tell me about yourself?' she pleaded. 'It's almost as if you're ashamed of something.' She paused, gazing into his brown eyes. 'What is it, Renard? Are your family poor, and are you afraid that if I find out, I'll no longer love you? You surely can't think that of me!'

Renard's arms tightened around her. 'No!' he said fiercely. 'I know you better than that, Lianne!'

'Then why the need for this stealth?' Lianne pleaded. 'It makes me so sad that we must meet like this, at night and in secret. I want to tell the whole world about you, Renard! If you would only come to Cerne, present yourself to my father –

'Ah, no.' Renard interrupted her

quickly, and suddenly there was a hard look in his eyes. 'I can't do that. Ever.'

Lianne stared at him, suddenly uneasy as she heard the change in his tone. He sounded bitterly angry. As though, without realizing it, she had stirred up some terrible memory from his mysterious past.

'I'm sorry,' she said. 'I didn't mean to upset you. I was only trying to –'

He stopped her with a kiss from saying any more. Then he drew her close, stroking her hair as she laid her head against his shoulder. 'There is a very good reason why I can't come to Cerne House and meet your family.' He released her, stepped back a pace and looked at her intently. 'Your father and mother wouldn't accept me. You see, there is an old connection – a very old connection – between my family and yours. And it's not a happy story.'

Lianne's lip quivered. 'But if it's so far in the past, why should it affect us now?'

'It does. Believe me. It was all such a

long time ago, and yet . . . your father would only need to see my face to know who I am. One look, and he'd turn me out and stop you from ever seeing me again.'

'He couldn't!' Lianne cried.

'Oh, he could. And he would. So I must stay away from Cerne, and we must go on meeting in secret. There's no other choice.'

No matter what Lianne said, no matter how hard she tried to sway him, Renard would not be moved. He wouldn't come to Cerne. Their love must remain a secret. And he would not explain why. Not yet. *Not yet.*

But Lianne was not content. How could she be, she asked herself, when her chance of happiness was being threatened by something from the distant past? If there had once been trouble between their families, Renard had had no part in it. Why should he be held to blame now? It was so *unfair.* Surely, she thought, even her father must understand that the past wasn't Renard's fault. If only Renard would come to Cerne! Together, they could make everything all right.

But Renard wouldn't change his mind, and it seemed there was nothing Lianne could do to persuade him.

Until, one stormy afternoon, she had a reckless idea . . .

Chapter Seven

LIANNE DIDN'T TELL anyone. Not even Gretala, for after their last argument she couldn't be sure that Gretala wouldn't be so afraid that she would run to Priddy with the tale. And that would ruin everything.

Lessons ended early that afternoon. The wind had been rising all day and was threatening to become a full gale, so Lady Cerne took pity on the girls' tutor and sent him home before the weather worsened. Gretala went to help Priddy, who was making a new batch of her famous winter cough-tonic in the kitchen, and Lianne slipped away to the turret room.

The wind was so furious that the turret seemed to rock like a ship. It flung dead leaves and twigs against the window, and when Lianne looked through the glass she saw that huge banks of clouds were massing in the sky. The sun was already blotted out, and the world looked grim and dangerous. With a shiver Lianne drew the curtain and lit a candle. Then she opened her linen chest and drew out Grandmother's necklace in its box.

The topaz winked like a cat's amber eye as she lifted it up. For a moment Lianne longed to put it on, fasten the clasp around her neck and admire herself in the mirror. But she resisted the temptation. She had another use for the necklace today.

Though he didn't know it, Renard himself had given her the clue. He had said, 'You only have to call, and I'll answer.' *Had* to answer, he had told her. As if the jewel had some power over him which he couldn't resist. Was that true? Lianne wasn't certain. But now, she meant to put it to the test.

She knelt on the bed and cupped the topaz in her hands, holding it close to the table where the candle stood. Tiny reflections of the flame sprang to life in the gem, and Lianne concentrated with all her will-power.

'Renard.' She whispered his name eagerly, secretively. 'Renard, where are you? Come to me, Renard! Come to me!'

The candle-flame quivered in a sudden draught, and a shadow seemed to move deep inside the jewel. Lianne tensed with excitement, for the shadow could, just *could*, have looked like a dark cloak . . . or black hair. Had Renard heard her?

'*Renard!*' She put every ounce of her concentration into the call. 'Renard, oh, come to me! You *must* come to me! Come now, to Cerne, to my father's house!'

Again she seemed to see the shadow in the topaz's depths. And now, in a tiny corner of her mind, she could feel something. A presence, faint but sure. Someone was there. *Renard* was there!

But Renard was resisting her. He didn't want to answer the call. He was afraid.

'There's nothing to fear, my love,' Lianne whispered urgently. 'Please, Renard, please – come to me. Answer me.' Her hands tightened on the necklace until the silver filigree dug painfully into her fingertips, and her resolve strengthened. He couldn't fight the power of the topaz. It bound him to her, bound him to do as she bade him. She drew a deep breath and spoke almost sternly. 'You *must* come, Renard. I love you, and I will you to come. *You must answer my call!*'

For one moment, just one, she glimpsed his face in the jewel. His eyes were filled with fear. Then, as quickly as it had appeared, the image fled, and at the same instant the tiny contact Lianne had felt with Renard's mind vanished.

She gave a gasp. Her breath blew the candle out, and as the turret plunged into gloom there was a fearsome rattling at the window, as if a wild animal had leaped to claw its way in. Lianne jumped, dropping the necklace and jolting backwards in fright – then her terror vanished as she realized it was only the wind hurling a new shower of debris at the glass. Not a demon; not something new and hideous conjured up by the topaz's magic to trick her. The face she had seen was Renard's. The presence she had felt was Renard's. She had made the summoning – and she knew in her heart that it had worked.

When would he arrive at the house? Lianne's heart began to pound with exhilaration. He *would* come, she was certain. An hour, perhaps? More? How far away was he now, and how long would the journey take him?

'Oh, Renard.' She picked up the necklace again and clutched it to her. 'Hurry, my love! Hurry to me! And when you are here, we'll see Father together. He won't turn you away. He can't – I won't let him! Everything will be all right, Renard. I just *know* it will!'

She put the necklace back in its velvet box and hid the box away in the linen-chest once more. Then she turned to her wardrobe. She would wear her finest clothes for him. She would be beautiful, and he would be proud of her.

Quickly, her pulse racing with joy and excitement, Lianne began to change her gown.

The light was fading fast, as though all the life were being drained out of the world. Lady Cerne had ordered the lamps and candles to be lit early, but no matter how much light there was in the house, it couldn't banish the shadows. They lurked in every corner, and as Lady Cerne came down the great staircase they seemed to close in around her like dark ghosts. The wind roared and rattled everywhere, echoing in the empty hall below and making the candles in their sconces dip and flicker, and the huge, stained-glass

window at the hall's far end was dulled to
dreary greyness.

Lady Cerne shivered, wishing there was
a curtain at the window to shut out the
grim day. She *hated* this house. It had
always made her nervous, ever since she
had first arrived here as a young bride.
However hard she tried she could never
shake off the impulse to look over her
shoulder wherever she went. And in
autumn, when the wind howled like this,
the uneasy feeling was so strong that
sometimes she *did* look back, half
expecting to see something . . . she didn't
dare imagine what . . . following silently,
horribly behind her.

Halfway down the stairs she paused,
wondering whether her husband was still
in his study. Lord Cerne spent much time
in there. He seemed to prefer being alone
with only his thoughts for company, and
Lady Cerne shivered again. They had
been so happy once, long ago, when they
were first married. But Cerne House had
worked its dark, cold spell on them both,

and now there seemed to be only sadness and fear. She sighed. Better not disturb Lord Cerne until dinner was announced. She would find Priddy instead, and see how the cough-tonic was progressing. That would help the time to pass.

She continued on down the staircase, then suddenly paused. There was a shadow in the hall below which didn't quite seem like the others. It looked too *solid*. And it was moving . . .

Suddenly there was a break in the clouds outside. The last rays of the setting sun broke through, and the great window flared into brilliance as though filled with flame. And the gory red light fell directly on to the strange shadow.

The shadow changed. One moment it was nothing but a shape of darkness; the next –

The boy's figure sprang to life out of the shadow. Lady Cerne saw the pale face in its frame of black hair, and the sudden swirl of the cloak. Dark eyes met hers, and a fire burned in them; a fire of bitterness, of pain – and of powerful, dreadful fury.

Lady Cerne knew that face. Not only knew it, but feared it to the core of her soul. And her voice ripped through the house like the sound of a banshee's wail as she screamed in terror.

There was an immediate hubbub, feet running, voices calling out, as the entire household came rushing to see what was the matter. Lord Cerne burst from his study, his face shocked – and as he raced out into the hall, he saw the figure of a boy.

'What's this?' Lord Cerne bellowed. 'Damn it, who are you? What are you doing in my house?'

Renard spun round, fast as a cat. As Lady Cerne screamed he had darted for the door, but Lord Cerne's shout made him turn. And as he saw the boy's face for the first time, Lord Cerne's own face went white.

'Ah, no . . .' Suddenly there was horror in his voice. 'No, *no*! You can't have come back! *You can't have come back!*'

Renard snatched at the door-latch. The door jolted open and the gale roared in, whirling a storm of leaves and dust before it. For a moment Renard's shape was silhouetted against the glare of the dying sun, and a wild aura seemed to blaze around him. Then, as though the wind had snatched him away, he was gone, and the door smashed shut.

Lord Cerne ran to the door and wrenched it open again. But the boy was nowhere to be seen. There was no fleeing figure running across the garden, nothing. He had vanished into the gathering night.

Then, from the stairs, a quavering voice called, 'Father . . .?'

Lianne had heard her mother screaming and had run from the turret room in alarm. She had just been in time to glimpse Renard as he bolted from the house, and her face was a mask of shock and dismay. 'Father, what's happened? What –'

'Lianne.' Lord Cerne's voice was so ominous that it froze Lianne where she stood. Very slowly, he paced across the hall floor, ignoring the servants who stood gaping in bewilderment. Lady Cerne was sobbing, covering her face with her hands; she seemed to be saying something but Lianne couldn't hear what it was. All she knew was that her father was advancing towards her, and in all her life she had never known him to be so angry.

'*Daughter*,' Lord Cerne said in a tone that shook with rage, '*what have you done?*'

Chapter Eight

THE GIRLS STOOD before the great table in their father's study. Lord Cerne himself sat behind the table, his face thunderous, while Lady Cerne had subsided on to another chair.

And on the table, between Lord Cerne and his daughters, was the topaz necklace.

Lianne and Gretala hadn't been able to lie to their father. Lianne had wanted to try, but at the last she was too overawed. Besides, nothing she could say would have made any difference, for Gretala had tearfully confessed the truth. The knowledge that they had exchanged the gifts Grandmother had given them would have been enough in itself to enrage Lord Cerne. But Gretala had told him everything – including the story of Lianne's secret meetings with Renard. Lianne could only admit what she had done, and she hung her head in miserable terror as she waited for the storm of wrath to break.

But it didn't break. Instead, Lord Cerne stared at her for a long time. Then at last, very quietly, he spoke.

'Daughter,' Lord Cerne said, 'you have been disobedient.'

Lianne bit her lip. 'Yes, Father,' she said in a small voice.

'You have also been foolish and reckless.'

'Yes, Father . . .'

'But –' Lord Cerne paused, and a new and awful note in his voice made Lianne feel as if something in her was turning to ice. She looked up. Her father's eyes were like flint. 'But,' Lord Cerne repeated, 'all that is nothing – nothing – compared to the greater wrong you have done. *For you have put us all in terrible danger!'*

Lianne was bemused. 'Danger?' she echoed. 'But Father –'

'Be silent!' Lord Cerne roared, and Lady Cerne spoke up quickly.

'Husband, she doesn't understand what she's done! She doesn't know the legend!'

At the word 'legend' Lianne drew a sharp breath. What did her mother mean? Was this something to do with the old quarrel between their family and Renard's?

She said desperately, 'Father, please – if there was once some trouble between us and Renard's family, then surely it is all in the past now?'

'Oh, no,' Lord Cerne glowered at her. 'It *was* in the past. But now it has come back. You have brought it back, Lianne.' He glanced at Lady Cerne. 'She must be told, wife. She must be made to understand what she has done.'

'But *what* have I done?' Lianne pleaded.

Her father reached out. His hand closed round the topaz necklace and he gripped it, as if he wanted to break the jewel in half.

'You have meddled, Lianne, with things that should have been left to lie in the darkness that spawned them. For with this necklace, and the power it contains, you have awoken the curse of Cerne!'

And, as Lianne and Gretala listened with growing, chilling fear, Lord Cerne at last told them the true story behind Grandmother's legacy.

Tezer, the head groom who loved to tattle, had been right – there *was* a curse on the family of Cerne. A curse that brought gloom and shadows to this house and all who lived in it. And it had all begun more than two hundred years ago.

'Our family was very far from wealthy in those far-off days,' Lord Cerne said. 'But one man – my ancestor – was determined to change his fortune. And so he made a bargain with a sorcerer who lived hereabouts; a loathsome but very powerful man. It was said that the sorcerer could turn day into night if he wished to; so surely a spell to bring riches would be nothing to him? The sorcerer agreed to the bargain. But there was a price.' He looked up. 'And the price he demanded was the hand in marriage of my ancestor's beautiful, auburn-haired daughter.'

The ancestor, Lord Cerne went on, was horrified by the idea of giving his beloved child to such a man. But the sorcerer was insistent. He became threatening, and Cerne was too afraid of his powers to argue. So he pretended to agree, and the bargain was struck. Within three years, the sorcerer promised, the family of Cerne would come into great wealth. They would build a fine house, own splendid lands, and Cerne himself would earn the title of Lord. And in three years and three days, the sorcerer would return . . . to claim his promised bride.

The sorcerer then turned to an iron-bound chest in his hall, and took something from it. This, he said, would be the key to the family's new riches. They must keep it safe always, for if it ever left their care they would be brought to ruin. And, the sorcerer added with a cruel smile, it would also be his betrothal gift to Cerne. The price for his daughter's hand.

'My ancestor looked at the object the sorcerer had placed in his hand,' Lord Cerne said. 'It was a necklace. A silver necklace set with a great topaz.'

Gretala made a little whimpering sound, but Lianne only stared as horror made her skin crawl. 'What happened . . .?' she whispered. 'Did . . . did the sorcerer return?'

He did indeed return, said her father. The family's fortunes had changed as he had said they would: Cerne House was built and the ancestor had become its very first Lord. Three years passed. Then, on the third day after that third year ended, a strange, black carriage drew up at the front door. The sorcerer had come for his bride.

'My ancestor pleaded with the sorcerer

to release him from the bargain,' Lord Cerne said. 'He offered him land, gold, anything, if he would only give up his claim. But the sorcerer would not listen. Cerne's daughter had been promised to him, and he meant to marry her that very day.' He frowned. 'At last there was a quarrel, and my ancestor declared that no power in the world would make him give his daughter into the clutches of such a monster. The sorcerer might do what he pleased: take his wealth away, anything, but he would *not* have the girl for a wife! The sorcerer flew into a rage, but my ancestor called up his men-at-arms and they drove the foul creature away.

'They thought they had heard the last of him,' Lord Cerne added darkly. 'But they were wrong. For that very night, in the midst of a great thunderstorm, the sorcerer used his magic to spirit the girl away.'

In a ferment of horror and grief, he said, the first Lord Cerne gathered his men together and went in pursuit of the sorcerer and his captive. They tracked them to the gloomy house where the sorcerer lived – and amid the lightening and thunder of the storm there was a terrible battle. The sorcerer used his evil powers against Cerne and his men, but at last even his strength wasn't enough against their numbers. He was mortally wounded, and as he lay dying, Lord Cerne rescued his daughter from the tower where she was imprisoned. As soon as she had been freed the men set fire to the house, and the party returned home in triumph.

That night there was a great celebration in Cerne House. With the sorcerer dead and his house destroyed, the family was sure that they had defeated his dark power for all time. But as midnight struck, an eerie light suddenly appeared in the hall. It was shining from the box where the topaz necklace was kept, and when the box's lid was opened, the family saw that the topaz itself was glowing as though it had come to life. As they looked in horrified amazement, the dead sorcerer's face appeared in the jewel. And then, from thin air, his voice spoke to them.

'*You believe you have defeated me,*' the sorcerer said, '*but you are wrong. For I will not rest until I have what is rightfully mine!*' The topaz glowed brighter, like fire, and the spectral voice continued. '*From this night onwards the house of Cerne will never be happy again until the promise you made to me is fulfilled. And that day will come, no matter how long I must wait. Take care, Lord Cerne – take great care! For if ever an auburn-haired daughter of your house should gaze into this jewel, I will return and claim her in place of the bride you stole from me. This is my promise to you – and my curse upon you all!*'

In the study, it was suddenly very silent. Lianne was staring at the necklace in her father's hand. She couldn't speak. Gretala was crying again, and Lady Cerne went to comfort her. But Lord Cerne only sat very still and looked at Lianne.

'Daughter,' he said, 'do you understand what you have done? Since that terrible day the necklace has been handed down through our family. We dare not rid ourselves of it, for fear of losing our fortune. But it has been an unbreakable rule that no auburn-haired girl born in this house may *ever* look into this evil jewel. Now, though, you have broken that rule, Lianne. You have looked. And the sorcerer has come back to fulfil his pledge. Renard – your precious Renard – is his ghost!'

Lianne's lower lip began to tremble. She didn't want to cry but had an awful feeling that she wouldn't be able to stop herself. Renard and the sorcerer, one and the same? It wasn't possible! Surely, she thought desperately, it wasn't! Renard wasn't evil! He was her beloved, her own, the boy she was destined to marry. This couldn't be true!

'Father –' she started to say desperately.

'No,' Lord Cerne interrupted sternly. 'You will say nothing, Lianne!'

But Lianne was too heartbroken to care. However her father might punish her for defying him, she *had* to speak, and rashly she rushed on. 'But, Father, this is wrong! Renard isn't a ghost, he's real! As real as I am! I've *seen* him, Father, I've talked to him! And – and you saw him, too. Tonight, in the hall before he ran away. He isn't a loathsome monster, he's young and handsome! How can he be an evil magician? There's been a mistake, a terrible mistake, I *know* there has!'

Lord Cerne didn't fly into a rage as she feared. Instead, he beckoned to her. 'Come here, Lianne. Stand beside me. I have something to show you.'

Nervously, Lianne moved around the table until she stood next to his chair. Her father picked up the necklace again.

'This jewel has one more secret,' he told her. With one finger he touched a little silver knurl above the topaz. To Lianne's astonishment the gem in its mounting swung back, revealing a compartment beneath like the inside of a locket. And in the compartment was a tiny picture.

'The sorcerer placed his own portrait inside the necklace,' Lord Cerne said grimly. 'Look at it. Look closely.' He held the jewel out. 'Do you recognize it, daughter?'

Lianne looked. And Renard's face gazed back at her.

Chapter Nine

'PLEASE, PRIDDY, *PLEASE!*' Lianne begged tearfully, 'Open the door. Let me out!'

Priddy's muffled voice came back to her. 'Now, girl, you heard what His Lordship said! You're to stay there until he and your poor mother say otherwise.' Then Priddy gave a loud sniff. 'And you should think yourself lucky that you haven't been whipped after what you've done! You'll have your supper in an hour or two, and I'll hear no more from you!'

Lianne heard the nurse turn away,

muttering, 'To think that such a child should bring ruin on us all . . .', and then her footsteps faded down the turret stairs. For a minute Lianne listened, then when Priddy was gone she sank to the floor and covered her face with her hands, weeping bitterly.

She had tried frantically to argue with her parents, to make them see that they were wrong. But they wouldn't listen, and at last Lord Cerne had lost his temper. She was to go to her room, he ordered, and be locked in there until he and Lady Cerne had decided what should be done.

Lianne knew that her father was very frightened. She had seen it in his eyes, a shadow like the shadows that gathered in the house. And now she knew why. Grandmother's necklace and the terrible legend. She hadn't wanted to believe it and had been ready to shout and scream that she *wouldn't* believe it. But the tiny portrait underneath the jewel had broken down her resolve. The face in the painting was so like Renard's that as she saw it she had felt as if someone had stabbed her to the heart. And her father believed that this was the face of the sorcerer. A creature of evil. A ghost from the past.

'But it isn't!' Lianne cried aloud. 'It can't be! Renard isn't evil! He isn't even a ghost – he's a boy, as real and alive as anyone, and I love him so much . . . Oh, please, somebody, help me!'

But there was no one to hear her and no one to answer. Only the gale, whistling mournfully round the turret and rattling the window. To Lianne's fevered mind it seemed that the gale was laughing cruelly at her, and she clenched her fists in helpless anguish. A *terrible* mistake had been made, and she had no power to put it right. Renard was no vengeful spirit come back from the dead! Even if the legend was true – and part of Lianne refused to believe that it was – then the awful resemblance between her beloved and the portrait of the long-dead sorcerer must be a horrible coincidence. They couldn't be one and the same. They *couldn't*!

Had Renard known about the legend? Was that why he had refused to come to Cerne House of his own free will? Lianne didn't understand how he could know, but she was certain that this was the reason for his fear. '*Your father would only need to see my face,*' Renard had said. And he was right, Lianne thought bitterly. One look, and Lord Cerne had believed that Renard was the ancient legend come to life. He was so wrong!

But now it was too late, and nothing Lianne could say or do would make her parents understand. They were furiously angry. Priddy was deaf to her pleas. Gretala was forbidden to come near her. And Renard . . . Renard wasn't here to help her make them all understand the truth.

'Oh, Renard!' Lianne turned her tear-stained face towards the window. 'I can't lose you! I can't bear it! Come back, come back . . .!'

All that night Lianne was alone in her turret room, without even Gretala for company. Priddy, when she bought a meagre supper, said that Gretala was to sleep in the little room next to her mother's tonight, and Lianne wouldn't be allowed to see her until Lord Cerne gave his permission. In the meantime, Priddy added, Lianne must stay here – and, if she had a single tatter of sense left in her head, she would think on the wicked thing she had done, and repent!

Lianne didn't argue with Priddy; in fact she didn't even answer her scolding. She simply sat with shoulders slumped, her face a picture of sheer misery. Then, when she had eaten what she could of the supper, she put on her nightgown and climbed into bed.

It was hopeless. She was trapped here, and couldn't escape. On a wild impulse she had thought that maybe she could tie her bed-sheets together, throw them out of the window like a rope and climb down them. But the turret was far too high; the sheets wouldn't reach to the ground and if she tried she would probably kill herself.

There was only one hope. If she could not run away to Renard, she *must* try to bring Renard to her once more.

All through the night Lianne stayed awake, picturing Renard's face in her mind and trying with all her will-power to call him back. But it was useless. Without the topaz, the magic couldn't work. And the topaz was locked away in her father's study where she could not reach it.

At last she had to admit defeat. She fell asleep but had hideous dreams, and when she woke in the morning her pillow was wet with tears. Priddy arrived soon afterwards, with a tray of breakfast that Lianne didn't want, and said ominously that Lord and Lady Cerne were on their way up to see her.

They arrived a few minutes later, and Lianne listened in growing horror as Lord Cerne told her what they had decided.

'You are to be sent away,' Lord Cerne said, 'for your own safety. You will go to the house of your mother's cousin, where the monster you have called up with your meddling cannot reach you.'

'No!' Lianne cried. 'Oh, Father, please –'

'*Silence!*' Lord Cerne was in no mood to be argued with. 'You will obey me, daughter! Perhaps you are too young to truly understand the evil you have brought upon this house. But it *is* an evil, and I mean to put an end to it. Your mother's cousin lives far enough away for the sorcerer's curse to have no influence on you. You will be safe there. And with you gone, the sorcerer can bring no more harm to Cerne.'

They left Lianne sobbing, and the key was turned in the lock of the turret door. Lianne was to stay in her room, Lord Cerne said, until all was ready for her departure. Arrangements would be made quickly, and she would leave in his carriage tomorrow morning.

One more day. Just one. Lianne's tears dried at last and she sat very still. She wouldn't give up hope. Somehow, *somehow,* she would escape. And when she did, she would search and search, and would not rest until she had found Renard.

At noon, Gretala was allowed to see Lianne. She entered the turret to find Lianne lying facedown on her bed. At the sound of her sister's footsteps Lianne looked up with tear-reddened eyes.

'Oh, Gretala, what am I to do? Father's going to send me away!'

'I know,' said Gretala. 'That's why he has let me come here, so we can have some time together before you go.' She bit her lip, then stared down at her shoes. 'I'm so sorry, Lianne. Sorry I told them everything.'

'You couldn't help it.' Lianne sniffed and wiped her eyes. 'If you hadn't owned up, I would have done. Father would have made me. But Gretala, I *can't* leave. I can't go away and forget about Renard, I couldn't bear that!'

Gretala was appalled. 'Lianne! You're not saying you still love him? After what Father told us about him?'

'But Father's wrong!' Lianne cried. 'Don't you understand? Renard and the sorcerer aren't the same person, they can't be! There's been the most awful mistake, but Father and Mother won't let me try to put things right!' She clenched her fists with frustration. 'I've got to find Renard. He'll tell them the truth, he'll make them understand.'

'But how can you? You're to leave in the morning, and –' Then Gretala stopped as she saw the look in her sister's eyes. She knew that look so well. Lianne had a plan. And, whether she liked it or not, Gretala was part of it.

She said, 'Oh, no, Lianne. No. I won't help you. Not this time. It isn't fair to ask me!'

'But there's no one else I can ask,' Lianne said piteously. 'Gretala, *please*. All you have to do is wait until there's no one around, get the key to this door and let me out.'

'*All I* have to do?' Gretala echoed. 'And if we're caught, what then? Father will whip us and send us *both* away!'

'He won't, for he won't catch us. Just lock the door behind me then put the key back, and no one will know it was you.'

'I can't,' Gretala said. 'I just can't.' But there was doubt in her eyes, and Lianne knew that she was going to win. Her will-power was so much stronger than Gretala's.

'Oh, Gretala,' she said cajolingly, 'You *can*!'

Lady Cerne and Priddy both took naps after lunch, as they always did, and Lord Cerne went to his study as usual, so it was easy for Gretala to steal the key to the turret room. Lianne was ready, wrapped in her warmest cloak with the hood pulled over her hair. She hugged Gretala excitedly and said, 'Wish me good luck!'

'I do,' Gretala replied. 'But . . .' She looked unhappily towards the window and, as if some demon knew what she was thinking, the wind howled anew. Gretala shivered. 'Lianne, I'm so scared!'

'There's no need to be. I'll be safe. Safe with Renard.' And she would find him, Lianne told herself. There was no doubt about it.

She kissed her sister quickly and skimmed down the turret stairs. With no candles lit, the corridors and landings of Cerne House seemed as dark and gloomy as a tomb, and Lianne forced herself not to shiver as she made for the front door. Past her mother's room (mustn't make a sound, for fear of waking her!), then to the staircase. Her heart leaped under her ribs as she tiptoed down, for she was terrified that at any moment her father's study door might open. But it didn't. She reached the hall, unhooked the latch of the door. From the top of the stairs Gretala was watching fearfully. Lianne turned, waved, then, like a ghost, was gone into the howling wind.

Chapter Ten

THE GALE HIT Lianne full on as she stumbled towards the wood, and she had to lean hard into it to stay upright. Twigs and earth and small stones flew at her, whirled by the wind, and though she tried to shield her face her cheeks were stung and cut by the flying debris.

But her resolve didn't waver. She didn't care what might become of her or how many hazards she might have to face. Finding Renard was all that mattered. And she *would*.

Cerne House was safely behind her, and she thought of her sister. Gretala was probably gazing out of an upstairs window now, striving to watch Lianne and torn between praying fervently for her safe return and terror that their father would discover what had happened. *Poor Gretala,* Lianne thought, and firmly pushed down a feeling of guilt. She *had* used her sister, quite shamelessly. But it was for such an important cause . . . and Lianne would make it up to her as soon as she could.

On she went. In the wood the going was easier, for the trees gave some shelter from the wind. It would be different when she came to the moor, Lianne knew. But she had to press on, for she was certain that she would find Renard at the ruined house.

Out on the moor the wind was like a rampaging wild beast. It took Lianne nearly an hour to reach the ruin, and by the time it loomed ahead she was staggering from exhaustion, her breath rasping from her throat in hard, painful gasps. But the sight of the jagged walls gave her comfort, and as she struggled the last few windblown steps towards them her hands reached out and she cried with all the strength she had left, 'Renard! Renard, I'm here! I've come to find you!'

But no voice answered her from the ruin. Perhaps, Lianne thought, he couldn't hear her over the moan of the wind . . . She swayed towards the flight of broken steps, hauled herself up to the empty doorway. *Where was he?*

'Renard!' The wind snatched her call and whipped it away with a sound like demonic laughter. 'Renard? Where are you?'

But still he didn't answer. Still he didn't appear. And when Lianne slithered down into the brambles and undergrowth beyond the door, and frantically combed the ruin in search of him, she found nothing. Renard wasn't there.

'Oh, no . . . oh no, *no*!' Lianne collapsed at last against the rough stones as she realized what a fool she had been.

Why should Renard be here at the ruin? This was their secret, night-time trysting-place, but it wasn't his home! And she didn't know where his home was. She didn't know where in all the world he might be.

Bitter tears began to stream down her cheeks and she sank to the ground, covering her face with both hands. She felt so *weary*. She couldn't go on, not back into the full force of the gale. She just needed to rest. Just wanted to *sleep* . . .

Lianne woke to find that the wind had dropped and the air was ominously still. And there was a strange darkness closing in.

With a sharp cry of alarm she sat up. How long had she slept? The sun couldn't be setting yet! But then she saw that the gloom wasn't caused by the coming of night. A vast bank of purplish-black cloud was moving slowly and menacingly in from the south-west. It had already blotted out the sun, and when Lianne looked fearfully towards it she saw that the clouds formed the dark and ominous shape of an anvil towering into the sky.

A thunderstorm. Lianne struggled to push down a surge of terror. At home, safe indoors, she didn't fear storms, but here in the open it was very different. Priddy said that the storm-devils which lived in thunderclouds watched for anyone out alone, and hurled bolts of lightning at them like an archer shooting arrows. And she told hideous tales of what happened to people and animals who were struck by the lightning . . .

Lianne scrambled to her feet. Whatever happened, she mustn't think about Priddy's stories or she would lose her nerve altogether. The storm hadn't begun yet. She still had some time. And if she could only find Renard, there would be nothing to fear.

The still air felt like a heavy blanket pressing down on her as she climbed back to the broken door of the ruin. On the steps she paused and gazed out at the moor. It seemed to stretch away endlessly in all directions, bleak and dangerous in the storm-light. Far in the distance Lianne heard a deep, echoing rumble, and a shiver shot through her. Thunder . . . she hadn't seen any lightning, so the sound must have come from a long way off. But the clouds were moving relentlessly towards her; the storm would surely break soon. And even if the sun wasn't setting yet, it was sinking low. Behind the grimly marching clouds the sky was turning blood-red, and through a narrow rift in the clouds a single ray of gory light lanced across the moor. The ray hurled Lianne's shadow out behind her like a black phantom, and the light seemed to stain everything around her to crimson.

Lianne's spirits quavered and sank. Renard could be anywhere – close by, or miles and miles away. What hope did she have of ever finding him on the moor? Surely, she told herself, it would be better to stay here at the ruin, for this was the one place where he might instead come searching for her.

If he wanted to . . .

She shivered violently and tried not to think about the possibility of him *not* wanting to, but it haunted her none the less. Did Renard think she had betrayed him? Or was he so afraid, now, of her father's fury that he would never return to find her? Or – most hideous thought of all – did he no longer love her?

'*No!*' She cried the word aloud, and the broken walls threw echoes of her voice back at her. She didn't believe that Renard no longer loved her. She knew him far better than that. And he must know that she would try to meet him, here, tonight. He would come, she was certain. All she must do was wait.

But waiting would not be easy. Lianne looked up at the sky and shivered again. The storm was marching nearer every minute, and the ruin offered poor shelter from the lightning and thunder. If the storm-devils should see her, there would be nowhere to hide from them –

She thrust that thought away, shaking herself angrily. Priddy was nothing but an old fool with her superstitions and dire warnings! Lianne had a clear choice: to brave the storm and its terrors or to run like a frightened rabbit back to Cerne House. Well, she told herself fiercely, clenching her teeth and trying to ignore the pounding of her heart, she would not run. No matter how bad the storm might be, no matter how greatly it terrified her, she would wait. No power in the world would make her give up now.

She found a place by the crumbling wall where she would have a little protection from the rain when it began. But though she tried to sit down and be patient, she couldn't. The rumblings of thunder were becoming angrier and more frequent, and her stomach felt as though it were twisting into knots with tension. Lianne almost wished the storm *would* break, for waiting like this, never knowing when the first great flash would come, was almost unbearable. But then she did see lightning, flickering in the distance, and changed her mind. Everyone at Cerne would be indoors now, and Lianne tried with all her strength not to want to be with them, safe under the house's roof.

The sky grew grimmer and grimmer, as if the storm were draining away and devouring all the light. The atmosphere felt very close and heavy now, and there was a dire stillness in the air. Lianne felt, unnervingly, that the entire world was holding its breath and waiting with her. And the sun really was setting now. Gloom was turning into deep darkness and the ruin seemed to be merging with the undergrowth, making everything indistinct and menacing.

Then something rustled a little way off.

Lianne froze and peered into the dark. But she could see nothing; the shadows were too deep now. What *was* that sound? Just a breath of wind stirring the tangle of greenery? Or something else? There were wild animals on the moor, she knew. And some were dangerous: wolves, wild pigs. They wouldn't attack two people together, but one girl, alone and unprotected, might be another matter.

Suddenly the rustling came again. Lianne's heart lurched wildly and she leaped to her feet, pressing her back against the wall. Whatever it was, it had moved. It was *closer.* Abruptly, horribly, it occurred to her that worse things than wild animals might be drawn to a place like this. Many ruins, it was said, were haunted by ghouls; creatures that crept out of the earth at night to seek and devour living human victims . . .

She made a small whimpering noise and instantly clamped a hand over her mouth, terrified that whatever was prowling might have heard her. And as she stared wide-eyed into the dark, it seemed that a long, lithe shadow moved a little way off. There was a sudden glimmer. *Eyes in the dark.* Then the shadow turned and, like something flowing over the ground, began to move towards her.

Lianne's hands clutched at the wall behind her as if trying to claw through the solid stone to escape. But there was no escape. She was trapped. *And it was coming closer –*

Then, so violently that the ruin seemed to shake to its foundations, a colossal flash lit the world as lightning exploded across the sky. Lianne screamed – and the scream became a shriek as the lightning's dramatic glare showed her the nature of the prowler in the night.

Thunder roared then with a huge, triumphant voice, and it drowned her cry so that he could not hear it. But in that one instant Lianne's terror had turned to joy, and she flung herself forward, arms outstretched, sobbing his name.

'*Renard!*'

Chapter Eleven

'**B**RING THAT HORSE out! Move, man, *move!*'
Lord Cerne's bellow rivalled the din of the thunder as he signalled furiously at Tezer, the groom. With a clatter of hooves and a shrill whinny the big bay mare came dancing from the stable. She was terrified by the storm but Lord Cerne would stand no nonsense; he snatched the reins from Tezer's hands and sprang into the saddle, wrenching the mare's head around. Another bolt of lightening lit his face as he looked back, and his voice rang out.

'Never fear – I'll find her!'

From the steps of Cerne House Lady Cerne watched him spur the mare to a gallop and vanish into the wild night. Then she ran back into the hall, where Priddy was loudly scolding Gretala. Gretala was crying, and Lady Cerne looked despairingly at them both.

'If Lianne is alive,' she said quietly, 'His Lordship will find her. We must wait for news and try not to think the worst.' Her mouth trembled. 'Gretala, how *could* you have been so reckless as to help her?'

'I didn't want to, Mother,' Gretala sobbed, 'but she pleaded and pleaded . . .'

'Well, there's nothing more to be said now.' It would all be said, Lady Cerne thought grimly, when her husband returned – with or without Lianne. 'For now, there's only one thing to be done. And that is to pray.'

Lianne's tears were mingling with the rain that poured down their faces and soaked their hair and cloaks as she clutched

Renard to her. Her entire body was shaking with emotion, and she knew that but for his encircling arms holding her close and safe she would have slid to the ground, unable to stand without support.

'Oh, Renard, Renard!' Her voice choked from her throat, barely more than a whisper. 'I was so afraid I'd lost you for ever! And then when I heard that sound, and saw the shadow –'

A blaze of lightning flared above their heads, and thunder eclipsed the rest of her words. As the echoes rolled away into the distance Renard said, 'I couldn't be sure it was you. I feared your father might have come here. Believing what he believes, don't you think Lord Cerne will want to find me – and destroy me?'

'He wouldn't come here,' Lianne said, trying to reassure him. 'He doesn't even know of this place!'

'But he does, my love.' Another flash of lightning showed Renard's face for a brief moment, and Lianne tensed as she saw his expression. 'Your father, like all his ancestors before him, knows what this house is.' He paused. 'Or rather, what it was . . .'

Slowly, as thunder howled again, Lianne turned her head and gazed at the ruin. What it *was* . . .?

'Oh, no . . .' she said. 'No, Renard!' She started to tremble violently. 'Not . . . not the sorcerer's house?'

'Yes. The same house that the first Lord Cerne burned so many years ago.'

'But the legend isn't true!' Lianne cried. 'It can't be! You're not evil, you're not a ghost!' Panic began to flower in her and she gripped his shoulders. 'Renard, my father is wrong! Tell me he's wrong!'

More lightning flickered, but it was further off and didn't truly light his face. And for the first time Lianne was afraid of him.

'Ah, Lianne,' Renard said at last. 'There is a story – but it's not the story your family has always known. I know the truth. And now I think it is time for me to show it to you.'

He stepped back from her but didn't release her arms. He was a silhouette in the darkness, and Lianne's heart began to pound with unease. What was he going to tell her? *What was he going to do?*

Before Renard could speak again, however, they both heard a new sound mingling with the noise of the storm. A rumbling; not thunder, but – *hooves.*

Lianne's eyes widened in horror. 'Horses! Renard, it must be my father – he's discovered me gone and he's coming to find me!' *Oh, Gretala,* she thought, *how could you have told them?*

'We must hide!' she added urgently. 'In the ruin – there's sure to be somewhere where Father won't see us!'

But Renard shook his head. 'No, Lianne. Now it's time to face him. And we'll do it together.'

The hoofbeats were drawing nearer. Just one horse – Lord Cerne hadn't brought other men with him, and Lianne was thankful for that at least. Another bolt of lightning streaked across the sky, and in the momentary glare she saw the mare and rider approaching. Fear overcame her and she clung to Renard, but he stood calmly, steadfast, staring into the dark. Then more lightning flashed, and as the following thunder rolled away a voice called out of the night.

'Lianne! I see you, girl! Don't try to hide from me!'

Renard answered for her. 'We are both here, My Lord.'

The mare whinnied, and Lord Cerne galloped the last stretch to the ruin, pulling up with a flurry.

'Lord Cerne.' There was a strange authority in Renard's voice. It stopped Lord Cerne in his tracks. 'My Lord, you are very wrong about me. I am not evil, and I wish you no harm. For, you see, the Cerne legend, as it has been handed down through your family, is not the truth.'

'Not the truth?' Lord Cerne fired back furiously. Thunder echoed his words. 'I know what the truth is! I know what you are trying to do! And I tell you now, sorcerer, you will not succeed!'

'Lord Cerne,' Renard said, 'I don't believe that you are cruel. I believe you love Lianne. I, too, love her. And for her sake, I ask you – beg you – to listen to me.'

Lord Cerne sneered. 'And if I do, what difference will that make? What proof can you give me that anything you say isn't a pack of lies?'

'I can prove that it is true,' said Renard. 'And I can prove it with far more than words.' He paused. 'I can show you the past, My Lord. I can show you how the curse was brought upon your house all those years ago. And when you know the truth, it may be that the curse can at last be lifted.'

Lord Cerne opened his mouth, then hesitated. He looked at Renard. Then he looked at Lianne. And Lianne, her hair draggled and her eyes miserable, gazed beseechingly back at him and said again, in a heartbroken whisper, '*Please,* Father . . .'

Suddenly Lord Cerne covered his face with his hands. Renard was right; he wasn't a cruel man. He loved his family, and wanted only to protect them from the evil that had beset Cerne House for so long. And if there *was* a way to lift the curse, he thought, then it could bring such happy changes to them all . . .

He looked up again and in the brief glow of lightning his expression had altered.

'I make no promises,' he said. 'But I will at least listen. Tell me your story, sorcerer, and prove it to me – if you can.'

Renard reached out and very gently touched Lianne's eyelids. 'Don't be afraid, my beloved,' he told her softly. 'I will show you and your father what really happened in those far-off days.' He turned again, and his dark cloak swirled around him, a wave of darkness that seemed to draw both Lianne and Lord Cerne into its folds.

'See with your own eyes,' Renard said, 'and with *hers* . . .'

Chapter Twelve

THE SOUND OF the rain seemed to swell around Lianne. Far, far away she heard a new roll of thunder beginning, and then –

The storm vanished. Rain was no longer falling on her, and instead of the racket of the storm there was a calm, deep silence. Lianne cried out, swaying backwards with shock; hands caught hold of her and steadied her. And, bewildered, she opened her eyes.

The ruin was gone. Instead, she and Renard stood in a long gallery above a hall. The gallery was draped with velvet curtains and tapestries, and soft, warm light shone from torches burning in brackets on the walls. Through seven tall windows in the hall below Lianne could see the flicker of lightning in darkness. So the storm was still going on. Or *a* storm . . .

She gasped at that thought and turned quickly to look at Renard. He seemed to know what she was thinking, for he said, 'Yes, there was a storm on that night, too. But there was no rain. Perhaps rain would have put out the fire.'

Lianne gazed around. 'This is . . . this is the ruin?'

'As it used to be.'

The sorcerer's house . . . but it wasn't the dark and evil place she had imagined. It was gracious, beautiful. And it felt *happy*, Lianne thought.

She remembered her father then, and turned to look for him. But he was not there. Renard, understanding, said, 'He was not a part of this story, Lianne, and so he is not with us now. He is still among the ruins, but he sees what we see, like a dream or a vision.'

She said in a very small voice, 'I don't understand.'

'You shall.' Renard slipped an arm around her, and with his other hand pointed towards the far end of the gallery. 'Look.'

She looked. Two people, a boy and a girl of about their own age, were coming towards them, holding hands. For a moment it occurred to Lianne that they looked familiar somehow. And then she saw them more clearly and her heart almost stopped.

The boy was Renard. And the girl . . . she was dressed in the clothes of a much earlier age, and her auburn hair was braided into two long plaits. But her face was Lianne's own.

Lianne made a tiny, frightened sound and clutched at Renard's arm. But she didn't speak. She only watched as the boy and girl walked slowly along the gallery.

They didn't seem to be aware of Lianne and Renard – the *other* Lianne and Renard. *Are we invisible?* Lianne wondered. *Or is this something else; something far, far stranger?*

Suddenly Renard stepped forward, drawing her with him. Before Lianne realized what was happening they had moved into the path of the approaching pair. They were about to collide with them, and Lianne made to protest, to give a warning –

A tingling shock went through her as she and the other Lianne met, touched – and began to merge. For one stunning moment Lianne saw an image of her own face as the other girl might have seen it, eyes wide and mouth open in astonishment. And at the same time she saw, too, the other Lianne with her plaits and gentle smile. Then –

She and Renard stood alone in the gallery. But Renard no longer wore his black, rain-sodden cloak. Instead he was dressed in the clothes that the other boy had worn.

Lianne looked down at herself. She saw the long, old-fashioned gown of the girl from the past sweeping around her feet and making a train behind her. And her hair swung in two long, red-brown braids to her waist . . .

'Renard, what – ?' But suddenly there was no need to ask the wild question, for she understood. She was herself, and yet at the same time she had become the girl from the distant past.

Memories came flooding into her mind then. Not her own memories but those of the girl from long ago. She knew why she was here. She had not been snatched away by the sorcerer. She had fled from Cerne House and her father – the very first Lord Cerne – because he would not let her marry the boy she loved. And that boy was the sorcerer's son, Renard.

Lianne knew now how wrong the Cerne family legend was. The sorcerer had never demanded her hand in marriage as the price for Lord Cerne's riches and good fortune. He had asked, instead, for a bag of gold when Lord Cerne became wealthy, and Lord Cerne had gladly paid him. But then Lord Cerne's daughter had met Renard . . .

'At first Lord Cerne was also pleased by the match,' Renard said. 'And my father gave the topaz necklace – with my portrait inside it – as a token of the betrothal. We should have been so happy.'

Yes, Lianne thought. For Renard and that long-dead girl had loved each other with heart and soul. 'But then,' she whispered softly, 'her father changed his mind . . .'

'Yes. He was newly rich, and he had great ambition. There was a neighbouring lord, with a grand estate and a great house and an ancient name, and he, too, had a son. Lord Cerne decided that it would suit him better if his daughter should marry for wealth rather than for love. So he sent word that I was no longer welcome at his house.

'My father and I went to Cerne House to plead with him, but we were turned away. Lord Cerne mocked us and called us arrogant fools to think that I was good enough for his daughter. He threw the topaz necklace at my father's feet and said, "Take back your worthless betrothal gift, for there will be no marriage." And then –'

Then, so the legend said, the sorcerer had used magic to spirit the girl away, Lianne recalled. But that was not the truth.

'Renard!' She turned to him, her eyes widening. 'Renard, I remember, I *remember* . . .'

He clasped her hands. 'Tell me what you remember,' he said.

'She – I – cried and wept and pleaded with my father. I loved you so much, and his betrayal broke my heart. But he wouldn't listen. So I ran away. I ran back here, to you, where I believed I would be safe. And when I arrived, your father took me in and was so kind to me. And you . . .' Quickly she put a hand to her throat as if expecting to find something there. But she found nothing, and her look became dismayed.

'The necklace,' Renard said softly. 'I fastened the topaz around your neck, to seal our promise to each other. And then I kissed you. Like this . . .'

But abruptly a sound interrupted them.

They broke apart and turned and looked down over the gallery rail.

A tall, grey-haired but still handsome man had entered the hall below them. He wore a long crimson robe and he was carrying a lantern, and Lianne's mind lurched as she recognized him – the sorcerer himself.

Renard's hands took a powerful grip on her arms and he swung her to face him again.

'Lianne,' he asked urgently, 'are you afraid?'

'No,' she said. 'While I'm with you, Renard, I'm not afraid!'

'Then listen to me. We must go deeper into the past together. To share the first Lord Cerne's daughter's memories is not enough. You must truly *become* her. And, together, we must live again through the events of that bitter time.'

A shudder went through Lianne. Live through it again . . . but there had been blood, and fire, and death . . . *And Renard – what had become of Renard on that fearful night?*

But even as the hideous fear grew in her, she knew she must have courage. For his sake. And she needed so desperately to know the truth at last.

She drew a deep breath and said, 'I'm ready.'

Then, as he had done before, Renard reached out and touched her eyelids with the tips of his fingers. There was a rush of darkness, a high, singing sound –

Chapter Thirteen

'RENARD! LIANNE!' THE sorcerer
hastened up the gallery stairs
to them. 'Lord Cerne is
coming with a force of armed men. He
means to take you back, Lianne, and he
will use any means he can to do it.'

As if from a long way off, she heard
herself saying, 'I won't go back! I won't
leave Renard!'

The sorcerer gazed seriously into her eyes.
'And I won't let your father force you. I have
promised you my protection. And unlike
Lord Cerne, I do not break my promises.'

'Father,' Renard said, 'we'll fight them! I can use a sword –'

'No, my son. Violence must be a last resort. I will try to reason with Lord Cerne, and only if that fails shall we fight. Now: the men are almost at the door. Wait here while I go and speak with them.'

They watched him go back down the stairs. As he reached the hall there was shouting outside, and moments later a thunderous knocking sounded at the door, echoed by another kind of thunder overhead.

As the sorcerer pulled the door open, Lianne saw that there were at least a dozen men outside, armed with swords and longbows. At their head was Lord Cerne himself. Her father . . . and yet not her father. For a moment the present-day Lianne and the long-dead girl seemed to clash within her mind and she shivered. Then the scene cleared again and she heard Lord Cerne shouting.

'Bring her out!'

'Lord Cerne, your daughter does not

want to return to you,' the sorcerer said. 'She loves my son. They are betrothed, and you gave them your blessing.'

'I withdraw my blessing! Do you think I care so little for my daughter that I'll let her throw herself away on a worthless husband?'

Lianne gasped. Fury rose in her. Her father wasn't doing this for her sake! All that mattered to him was increasing his own fortunes by forcing her into a wealthy marriage!

Suddenly she couldn't control her rage, and she screamed out, 'Father! I love Renard, and I will marry no one else!'

Lord Cerne heard her. Shouldering his way roughly past the sorcerer, he strode into the hall. Menacingly, he said, 'You will obey me, girl, or I will carry you home by force.' He swung round and beckoned. 'You men – to me!'

'*No!*' Lianne screamed. But even as she did so, Lord Cerne's men-at-arms came bursting through the door and into the hall. The sorcerer cried out in protest and tried to bar the way. But he was knocked aside, and like a tide the men surged towards the stairs with Lord Cerne leading them. They reached the gallery – and Renard stepped into their path.

Lord Cerne scowled contemptuously at him. 'Get out of my way, boy,' he said threateningly.

'I will not!' Renard's dark eyes were blazing with bitter anger. 'Lianne has chosen to be mine!'

There was an ominous metallic rattle as Lord Cerne drew his sword from its sheath. 'Move aside!'

'Father, *NO*!' Lianne shrieked. She flung herself forward, trying to push Renard aside and out of reach of Lord Cerne's blade. Renard shouted her name; she felt his hands grab hold of her, then suddenly he was pulling her away and they were running desperately along the gallery.

'*Lianne!*' Lord Cerne shouted in outrage.

Lianne paid him no heed. Hatred was

choking her – hatred for her father, for his cruelty and greed and selfishness. She heard the thud of booted feet as the men-at-arms started in pursuit, and she tried to run faster. But suddenly she realized that there was no escape. There was no door at the end of the gallery. They would be trapped!

And then, to her horror, she realized what Renard meant to do. For on the gallery wall at the far end, a shield and two crossed swords hung.

Her voice rose in shrill despair. 'Renard, you can't fight them! You'll be outnumbered – they'll kill you!'

She snatched at his arm, struggling to drag him back as he reached up for one of the swords. But Renard wouldn't heed her.

The sword came clattering down; he grasped it, hefted it, and swung round in time to meet Lord Cerne head-on.

Lord Cerne saw the sword in Renard's hand and snarled with fury. His own blade came up, and metal clashed with a terrible din and a shower of sparks as the two weapons met. Renard staggered under the force of Lord Cerne's blow, but he managed to turn the sword aside and shouted frantically over the balcony.

'Father! Use your powers – if you love us, use them, and help us now!'

Lianne heard the cry of something in a strange, high-pitched language, and suddenly the whole house seemed to shake. Then, with no warning, a bolt of silver light exploded from the sorcerer's fingertips and hurtled towards the gallery. It seared between Lord Cerne and Renard, and Lord Cerne reeled back with a yell, losing his balance and sprawling on the gallery floor. A second bolt followed, missing one of the men by a hair's breath, and shouts of fear echoed through the hall.

'Curse you!' Lord Cerne roared. He was upright again, and Renard, pushing Lianne behind him, backed towards the wall. 'I'll send you to a place from where you can never return!'

As he spoke the last words Lord Cerne lunged at Renard again – and suddenly everything seemed to erupt into mayhem. Wild, disjointed images flashed through Lianne's mind – men pounding towards the gallery stairs, her father's sword swinging, Renard's face. She heard herself screaming, heard the sorcerer's voice calling out again in that eerie tongue, felt more bolts of energy flying through the hall, crackling and exploding like lightning.

'*Oh, help him, help him! Help Renard! Don't let him die for me!*'

Lianne had a momentary glimpse of the sorcerer's face, white and stricken, as he tried to divide his attention and power between his son and the men who were coming at him to attack. She saw the blur of an arrow's deadly flight – and saw it strike the sorcerer and pierce his heart.

Then suddenly she felt Renard's arm go tightly around her, felt the warmth of his body against her . . . and felt another warmth, for blood was welling from beneath Renard's ribs, turning the fine white linen of his shirt to crimson. And then she saw that there was blood on Lord Cerne's sword.

'Father, no . . .'

But Lianne's cry went unheard. Her father raised his sword one last time –

Renard fell without a cry, without even a single sound. His hands reached out to her and his fingers touched her throat. The topaz necklace was there, somehow it was there, and for one moment Renard tried to hold it, as though it had the power to link him with Lianne. But then his hands slipped away, and Lianne was carried screaming from the house and out into the storm where the other men were waiting.

She saw torches burning brightly in their hands, the flames leaping hungrily. She heard her father give the order to set fire to the house. And as she was borne away on Lord Cerne's horse, she saw the grim orange-red glow rising and growing stronger as the house began to burn. And at her throat, the topaz began to glow with a savage answering fire of its own . . .

Then suddenly the scene seemed to shiver and fade. An agonizing sensation tore at Lianne's mind, as if she were somehow splitting apart. For a moment she was herself again, then the other Lianne, then both at once. Then lastly, eerily, she seemed to become nothing and no one at all, for she was gazing down, as though from a great height, on the blazing house. And she could see through the fire, through the roof and walls, to the gallery . . . and Renard. He wasn't dead. She could still hear his voice. *'I can do no more for you, my beloved. But I make you a last promise. I swear to you, my Lianne, that my soul will not rest until I come back to you. And when I do, we will never be parted again.'*

The scene was beginning to fade, and Renard's voice was fading with it. But still Lianne heard his final words.

'I am not a sorcerer as my father was. I know no magic as he did. But I have another kind of power. The power of love.'

Darkness came down like a soft wing.
Renard and the house and the fire were
gone, and Lianne felt rain drenching her
as she stood, eyes closed, among the ruins
on the moor.

Chapter Fourteen

THE STORM HAD lessened, though lightning still flickered and the thunder still grumbled. But Lianne didn't fear it now. For she had truly been reunited with her love at last, and would never be afraid again.

Whether she really had been that Lianne of the past, or whether the long-dead girl's spirit simply lived on in her, she didn't know. But it didn't matter, for whatever the truth, they were one soul now. Renard's dying promise had come true. And the power of love, which was the

magic of the topaz necklace, had been
fulfilled.

'Oh, Renard . . .' Her voice was
breaking. 'All those years you waited, and
you were true to your promise. And my
father –' Bitterness and fury surged in her
and she turned suddenly to where Lord
Cerne stood a few paces away. She started
to cry, 'How could you – ?' but stopped as
she realized that he was not the same Lord
Cerne who had wronged them. The past
had slipped away. This was reality. This
was *now*.

And her father was weeping.

She knew then that he had seen it all as
she and Renard had seen it. The betrayal.
The murder of the sorcerer and his son.
The burning house. And he had heard
Renard's last vow . . .

Renard, too, turned towards Lord
Cerne, and spoke. 'The topaz necklace
was my betrothal gift to her,' he said. 'And
before I died, I willed the power of my
promise into the jewel. Since that night,
Cerne has been a house of fear and

shadows. But now Lianne and I are reunited. The wrong has been put right, My Lord. And the curse is gone.'

Lord Cerne stared at him through the falling rain. 'Before you died . . .' he whispered. 'What are you, Renard? A ghost?'

'Perhaps. Or perhaps something stranger. I don't know what I have become. All I can tell you is that I have lived – in a way – through all the years since that night. Waiting to find Lianne once more. And now . . .' Slowly he turned to look at the girl by his side. 'Now, I have found her.'

Lianne gazed back at him. She wanted to go with him. She longed so much to *be* with him, now and always, that the yearning was tearing her soul apart. But what would it mean for them both? What would it *mean*?

'It will mean,' said Renard, knowing her thoughts as if she had spoken them aloud, 'that we can no longer live in this world as we have done. What we will become, and where we will go, are questions I have no power to answer. But we will be together, Lianne. And I believe in my soul that we will be happy.'

Lord Cerne said helplessly, 'Lianne –' But Lianne did not hear him. She and Renard stood very still. Their arms were around each other and they were gazing into each other's eyes.

Then, softly and gently, Lianne spoke.

'I will go with you, my love.' She reached up to touch Renard's lips and felt his smile take form beneath her fingertips. 'Nothing matters but you. I've found you again, and I will be with you for ever. She turned to Lord Cerne. 'Father, will you give us your blessing?'

Lord Cerne's eyes filled with sorrow, for he knew what such a blessing would mean. If Lianne went with her beloved – if he let her go – then he and his family would never see her again. Yet though they would grieve for her, she would be happy. It was just, and right.

He said, 'My dear daughter . . . your

mother will mourn you, and I . . .' He made a little gesture, too abashed to speak openly of his emotions. 'But perhaps Cerne will have light again where there has been so much darkness.' He wiped his eyes. 'Yes, Lianne. I give you both my blessing.'

Lianne ran to him and embraced him, and Lord Cerne kissed her awkwardly but lovingly, knowing that it was for the last time.

Lianne took his hand. 'Kiss Gretala for me, Father. And Mother too, and Priddy . . . tell them that wherever I go with Renard, I will always love them. I will always love you all.' She smiled, and her face was radiant.

There was a shimmer of lightning in the sky overhead. For a moment the ancient, ruined house showed stark and strange against the sky. Then the lightning was gone. And where Lianne and Renard had stood, only the rain fell, pattering and steady, on the empty ground as thunder rumbled across the moor.

*

For a very long time Lord Cerne stood alone in the rain. He tried to tell himself that a man should not weep, but he wept none the less. Cerne House had shut out love for so long, but Lianne had broken the spell. At last his family was free.

Some time later, very slowly, he moved to where his mare was tethered and waiting. The storm was fading now. The rain was stopping. Soon, a new day would begin. There was a story to be told, and much to be done. And one of the first things he would do, Lord Cerne told himself, was have a portrait painted. A tiny portrait of Lianne, to be placed inside the topaz necklace together with Renard's. That way, no one would ever forget the boy and the girl whose love and courage had lifted the shadows from the house of Cerne.

The mare plodded slowly away from the ruin, back across the moorland path towards the wood and home. The rain ceased and there was no more thunder, only a calm, deep silence. Then, when the moor was empty, the clouds began to clear and the moon shone through. Silver light showered down on the old, broken walls, and moonbeams danced among the brambles. And – though it might have been an illusion – it seemed that something else moved there, too. Not quite shadows yet not quite real. Two figures, hand in hand. There was a swirl of a dark cloak. A flick of red-brown hair. And, faint in the quiet of the night, the sound of a girl's bright laughter.